Smyrna in Flames

Smyrna in Flames

A Novel

HOMERO ARIDJIS

Translated by Lorna Scott Fox

Mandel Vilar Press   Dryad Press

Publisher's Cataloging-in-Publication Data

Aridjis, Homero
Subjects: Asia Minor Catastrophe; Greco-Turkish War 1921-1922; Refugees-
    Izmir (Smyrna) Turkey; Greeks-Turkey-History 20th Century;
    Armenians-Turkey-History 20th Century; Massacres-Izmir (Smyrna)
    Turkey; Religious Intolerance-Christian Genocide-Turkey-History 20th
    Century
ISBN: 9781942134756. (English Language Edition)
LCCN: PQ7297 A8365 S86 2021

Printed in the United States of America
21 22 23 24 25 26 27 28 29 / 9 8 7 6 5 4 3 2 1

Mandel Vilar Press
Simsbury, Connecticut, USA
and
Dryad Press
Takoma Park, Maryland

www.americasforconservation.org | www.mvpublishers.org

For my father, Nicias Aridjis Theologos,
who survived the Asia Minor Catastrophe

All Olympus will be destroyed,
the white marbles of Poseidon
and the violated bodies of living Aphrodites
will roll down Smyrna's streets.

HIEROS LOGOS OF THE ELEUSINIAN MYSTERIES

Whoever hates mankind also hates his gods.

STATEMENT FOUND ON A WALL IN SMYRNA

The myth does not belong to me;
it comes from my mother.

EURIPIDES

Smyrna in Flames

A man was wandering, homeless and penniless, through the streets of Smyrna. With the map of the doomed city in his head, he felt like a stranger in his own body. The month was September, the year, 1922.

In his memory realities and dreams could not be reconciled; the days did not match up: the distance between his bygone self and his present self shrank with every step that brought him deeper into the city, deeper into his past.

The neighborhoods were familiar and yet something fundamental had changed there; small but great disparities, imperceptible at first sight, emerged like a face in the shards of a broken mirror.

He felt as though the person returning to adolescent haunts was another, at once another and the same, as Heraclitus of Ephesus would say, the philosopher who also said that the upward path and the downward path are the same.

He could have paraphrased that thought as follows: The street that goes up to happiness and the street that goes down into misfortune are the same; the only certainty is that I, an expatriate in my homeland, am invisible to everyone.

His body felt more of a burden than ever, skinny and undernourished; for during his last years in the army he had seemed old and pinched, and indeed disheartened. But his face was smooth, not only because of his youth but because his beard was sparse.

As he walked among the orphan mass of refugees, his face was peculiarly his own: following Tolstoy he thought that every refugee was unhappy in his own way, depending on the attitude to life instilled in him as a child.

"Then the defeated, dusty, ragged Greek soldiers began to arrive, looking straight ahead, like men walking in their sleep." So the American consul, George Horton, described the scene. "In a never-ending stream they poured through the town toward the point on the coast to which the Greek fleet had withdrawn. Silent as ghosts they went, looking neither to the right nor to the left. From time to time some soldier, his strength completely spent, collapsed on the sidewalk or by a door."[1]

Nicias knew that the troops who were taken into houses and given civilian clothes would be safe, unlike those whose tattered uniforms would betray them to the Turks as Greek soldiers.

Others, overjoyed to be back in Smyrna, reveled by way of hands, mouth, nose, and eyes in the tactile, palatable, olfactory, and visual feast the city offered. Above all they rejoiced in the sight of the sea.

Undeniably he was, like them, a man of exodus, a fugitive soldier who after years of fighting in the Greco-Turkish war had joined thousands of refugees from Asia Minor in their headlong stampede to the coast.

Born in 1900 in Tire, the town of fig trees, now in enemy hands, he was part of the vanquished army being chased by the Turks from the heart of ancient Ionia to the northern shores of

---

[1] George Horton, *The Blight of Asia: An Account of the Systematic Extermination of Christian Populations by Mohammedans and of the Culpability of Certain Great Powers: With the True Story of the Burning of Smyrna* (Indianapolis: Bobbs-Merrill, 1926), 119–120.

the Aegean. There were no serpents in the paradise from which he was being expelled; there were only men, hence his flight from pillar to post through the razed towns of Asia Minor.

Nicias was the name of the man who now roamed the city founded at Bayrakli. Occupied by the Greeks at the beginning of the first millennium BC, it was originally an Aeolian settlement, then Ionian, and was rebuilt by Alexander around Mount Pagus.

Alone with his shadow near the Fountain of Sighs, Nicias suddenly saw a Turkish soldier riding a red horse through the fields of Bournabat, brandishing a rifle with a bayonet fixed to the barrel.

Soon afterward he made out a galloping white horse in a cloud of dust. Its rider fired jets of blazing fuel into the bushes from his portable flamethrower, as if to test its destructive power.

Behind him came a black horse. The Turkish officer had a Mauser in his hands and a Luger in his belt. The *chettes* surrounding him, uncouth, malignant irregulars, looked impatient to go into action.

Last appeared a yellow horse mounted by a commander all in black, like an effigy of death. He was a one-man arsenal equipped with machine gun, grenades, pistols, and flamethrowers. His fez, bearing the likeness of Mustafa Kemal, was a black stain.

The horsemen thundered through a field of Oriental poppies. Above their blue-green lobulated leaves the blooms glowed red in the evening sun, crushed beneath the horses' hooves only for a moment, soon lifting their heads. All this when white Smyrna's back was turned.

"Blood-colored poppy, scarlet goddess, so drugged that your own shadow can't follow you to the edge of delirium," chanted a Turk in a nasal voice, splayed out in the sand.

Neither the smell of the dead soldiers nor the sight of horses that had fallen from a bridge seemed to perturb the Turkish riders. They ignored the pearly moon and the sun rolling on the horizon like a severed head.

But what affected Nicias most was not the movement of Turkish cavalry columns streaming silently towards the city; it was seeing the bell ringer of St. Stepanos Cathedral on his knees, about to be beheaded by a Turkish horseman bearing down on him with saber outstretched.

Nicias walked like a somnambulist under the canvas canopies of Frank Street. He was thinking about what he'd just seen, and about his uncle Aristides, killed by the Turks, and about his brother Kostas, who had remained in Tire to confront them, with predictable results.

In such a mood the shopping district, with its flaunting of luxury fabrics, expensive watches, and imported confectionery, struck him as not only inappropriate but downright obscene.

As though in a recurrent dream, the men and women of the city had flocked here in their ghostly garb. Hailing from different neighborhoods and social strata, those whom death would shortly seize were delighting in the superfluous trinkets on display. They were all here, like a roll call of death: the candidates for deportation and the young girls condemned to be defiled;

from the trolley and train drivers to the plumber, the carpenter, the doctor, the teacher, the prostitute, the flower seller, the tramp, and the deaf child who talked with her hands; from the peddlers of carpets, figs, almonds, tobacco, and raisins, and the employees without a job—not because they had been fired, but because their workplaces no longer existed—to the immigrants in this land of emigrants. Not one of them seemed to understand the gravity of events; all stood dreamily on the edge of the abyss with a smile on their lips.

Nicias knew the Sephardim of the Jewish quarter by their family names: Aguilar, De Juan, Fonseca, Sánchez, Santamaría, Galante, Zacuto—expelled from Spain, survivors of the Inquisition, ready for imminent exile, they spoke Greek, Turkish, and Ladino. Their bookshops contained volumes of Heraclitus, Herodotus, and Homer, and sometimes miniatures illuminated with scenes from Genesis, or a handwritten Haggadah from medieval Spain.

The ex-soldiers (like himself), the refugees, the displaced and the uprooted, reminded him of foreigners in transit, infants roaming the hostile streets with dismay written on their faces.

"Don't turn around. You're being followed. As a onetime captain in the Greek Army, you're on a liquidation list. I'm Calliope, Eurydice's friend. Keep walking."

"Who?"

"Calliope."

Nicias slid a sideways glance at the young woman in a white peplum, who worked in a textile store. The pale face, the eyes violet as bruised figs, had changed little since he'd last seen her.

"How did she know I was back?"

"She saw you in the crowd."

"In the crowd?"

"Yes, from the window of a safe room."

"Why didn't she come down to say hello?"

"She followed you in the street."

"And then?"

"She was afraid to give you away, so she didn't approach. Turkish agents are on your tail; it might have put you in danger."

"Am I such a menace?"

"She's active in the underground, like me."

"Where can I see her?"

"In the Greek cemetery, in an hour. Is that alright?"

"Tell me where."

"At the Andrakis family mausoleum. Now go. Don't turn round." Calliope melted back into the crowd.

The sound of Eurydice's name filled Nicias with longing and nostalgia. They had been close throughout their school years, and the desire to see her once more had goaded him forward in Thessaly, Thrace, and Marmara. Smyrna now bore the shape of her face. He recalled what she'd said one day as they were walking through St. Anne's Valley: "I have put on a mantle made of pieces of ancient mythologies. Cloaked in these spells I advance barefoot towards the assassin who lies in wait, armed to the teeth, around the next corner."

* * *

IL SERAGLIO

A poster for the Smyrna Theater announced Mozart's Turkish-set opera, featuring such characters as the English maidservant Blonde and the Muslim overseer of the Pasha's harem, Osmin. Nicias thought little of Turkish harems, stocked as they were with Greek and Armenian girls; they could be his own neighbors, his sisters.

Standing in front of this building, modeled on its Paris counterpart, whose circles were still—he imagined—echoing with applause for a past performance of Verdi's *Rigoletto*, he felt sick, as if the comic lightness of the Austrian composer's work were churning the rubble of his ruined life inside him. Especially because the world of soloists and arias distracted attention from the aggression of the Turkish army with its tactical offensives and retreats, not to say from the catastrophe that was coming down on Smyrna like a dense rain of unsieved flour.

The glimpse of Calliope evoked in his mind the flower-filled Bournabat garden where she used to take tea with her English employer. He thought of the bicycle races, the Mersinli *allée*, the mansion of Ioannis Kanas—benefactor of the Evangeliki and the Greek Hospital—and the palatial villas of Levantine families like the Girauds, whose Oriental Carpet Manufacturers company employed 150,000 people; but these images also compounded his misery, and the landmarks of old Bournabat hung like a dead weight on his shoulders. He headed for the Greek Cathedral of Agia Fotini not to pray, but to find somewhere to sit or to stretch out and sleep.

"Ad ve Soyadi." A Turkish officer barred his way, demanding his name.

"Kyriakos Melisurgos," he lied.

"Yurttaşlık."

"I am a Greek."

"Pasaport."

"Lost it."

"Where have you come from?"

"Smyrna."

"Where are you going?"

"Smyrna."

"There is no more Smyrna. There is Izmir."

The officer showed him a Baedeker where the word "Smyrna" above the street plan had been crossed out, and "Izmir" written in its place.

"I am in Smyrna," said Nicias, and sprinted into the throng.

The officer shouted behind him: "Stop that man, he's carrying a fortune under his rags!"

General Georgios Hatzianestis lay without moving on a bed, convinced his legs were made of glass and would shatter to pieces if he put his weight on them. The sunbeams dancing on the ceiling of his cabin seemed like messages from heaven, and since he believed he had perished in the battle of Afyon, he saw no point, as a speaking corpse, in issuing orders to moribund generations and vanquished subordinates.

The commander-in-chief of the Greek forces, having directed the campaigns against the enemy from the deck of his yacht berthed in Smyrna's harbor, had received word of his army's casualties and defeats with a wild, unhinged stare, more befitting an inmate of St. Simeon's asylum than a general in charge of the war against the tyrant Mustafa Kemal, the bane of the Greeks and the boon of the Turks.

He had begged the messengers bringing news from the front to close the door softly, or else his feet might break and he would find himself on the floor, like a statue in smithereens. Obsessed by his limbs, as frangible as a crab's, he found himself incapable of taking the smallest step, let alone of designing a counteroffensive that might stem the enemy advance. The Turkish forces, secretly equipped by the French and the Italians, had already won the battle of Dumlupinar and turned Asia Minor into hell on earth.

While Hatzianestis was busy repairing his villa—between lavish meals in a waterfront restaurant, issuing instructions to his chiefs of staff from the table—thousands of exhausted, famished, dispirited Greek refugees and troops continued arriving in Smyrna, with the manifest purpose of reaching the sea. But they found no relief in the city, only despair as they were ferociously attacked by Turkish soldiers armed with rifles, daggers, and machine guns, patrolling the city on foot, on horseback, and in military trucks.

Travelers in real life, the displaced continued to arrive. They sought a mother or a brother in abandoned or wrecked houses; the only news they got was of relatives who had died or gone away, military defeats, the bankruptcy of the Greek state, and desertions such as that of King Constantine, who had packed his bags and returned to Athens. The most dismaying news of all was that General Nikolaos Trikoupis, lately appointed to command the Greek forces in Asia Minor, had been captured by the Turks. In other words, the Greek Army had gone from being led by a madman to being led by a ghost.

Like existential orphans, the refugees made for the harbor with children, pets, and bundles in their arms, trying to protect their biological or material belongings and yet unable to protect themselves. Some, their faces still powdered by the white dust of plains and steppes, kept up a constant keening for the relatives who had succumbed along the way.

Walking down the hospitals street, from the Armenian quarter to the Greek quarter, then on to the Frank quarter, passing St. Stepanos Cathedral, the churches of St. Nikolaos, St. Demetrios, St. Catherine, and St. Polycarp, and St. John's Cathedral, Nicias said to himself: "How many Roman Catholic, Armenian Catholic, Greek Orthodox, Gregorian Orthodox churches there are, how many Anglican and Protestant temples there are in Smyrna. But as the saying goes, 'The Saracens came and gave us a thrashing, because God protects evildoers when they outnumber the righteous.'"

Standing before the bay, Nicias tried to remember where he'd lost his army knapsack, whether he left it carelessly on some rock or abandoned it by the wayside for being too heavy or too empty. Either way, it was not worth the risk of falling into the hands of the Turks and being robbed or murdered just for the sake of a worn pair of shoes, a green shirt, a rifle with no ammunition.

At the harbor, the refugees were soon disappointed: the ships that could have taken them away had already weighed anchor, and those still moored to the Quay were intended for duties other than passenger transport. Crowds occupied the beaches and docks, camping out on burning sands and rocks bathed in the sun's largesse, but without a crumb of bread to eat.

Nicias saw a little girl who in such circumstances was the envy of all the other children because her mother gave her a chocolate bonbon, and before their eyes she dug her fingers with relish into the soft fondant while a tiny piece of it melted in her mouth.

Lookouts on the rocks kept an eye on the movements of the Turks in case the alarm had to be raised. Boys played with shells and petals they found along the shore, unaware of the danger. Mothers nudged daughters' lips with empty cups, and the whole scene evoked the peaceful course of an ordinary day. But it was not what it seemed—death stalked the orphan throng, from the center to the periphery.

Nicias felt like two men here: one who walked the present city, and one who remembered himself in the city of the past; one who lingered in now-irretrievable situations, and one who sought a way out of the encircling present. The disc of the sun appeared double, one representing the earthly hell, the other a metaphor for the eye. And he, in the midst of this collective helplessness, like a man outside of his bodily envelope, felt as fragile as a snail without a shell.

As a teenager Nicias had spent so many afternoons, mornings, and evenings in the Greek quarter that he knew the shapes of its windows by heart, and where the shadows fell at different seasons of the year. But now, after so many years of absence, the doorways appeared unwelcoming, indeed hostile, shut fast against his refugee hands.

Beneath the silken dresses that swathed the forms of the Smyrnean girls he sensed blank indifference to his unkempt garb. And although the houses seemed to preserve their facades of yore, something about them had changed without changing. Internally, so to speak, the minute shifts were almost imperceptible; something had altered, not only in their external aspect but also within. Change had overtaken some part of their being, just as it had in him.

During the war against the Turks he had dreaded being surprised by death in an ambush, on a rickety bridge, in a squalid alleyway, or in some godforsaken village, and he even came to regret the waste of his youth in the savagery of this ethnic-religious conflict. A good son, a good brother, a good Greek, he had never ceased to worry for his loved ones and his country, afraid the Turks would attack Tire and kill his parents and brothers or abduct his sisters. Since he had spent his youth far from home and his family had more than once given him up for dead, he had grown accustomed to being absent, to being a dead man. And now he was wandering around Smyrna like a stranger, fearful that his absence could materialize, not because he willed it but because he might be killed by a Turk.

He felt invisible in those streets, in the most unbearable sense of the word: invisible to the point of nonexistence. His invisibility was deliberate as well as circumstantial, for in order to be invisible to others he first had to be so to himself. And since conspicuousness had its perils, to go unseen made him feel more secure. To go unnoticed was his safe-conduct to survival, for it was dangerous to be Greek and male in this place, where enemies crouching behind doors and walls might shoot or knife him at any moment. He felt like a nothing surrounded by fear, and yet this nothing also had pressing material needs: to eat, to drink, to urinate, to defecate, to sleep.

The camouflage afforded by the crowds by no means offered a free pass, only a shared randomness. He had spotted agents of the police chief, a death squad that was shadowing him through the streets and squares, which meant he was on a list of military targets for assassination.

Aware of being watched, he decided to master his impulses and behave like just another refugee, pretending to be unaware of the tails, yet ready to confront them. But when he thought to give them the slip by heading for the docks, they doubled up: instead of two there were four, and now their weapons were not hidden but in plain view.

On the pier, gazing at the merchant vessels and the warships of the so-called allies, he made a private vow: he would survive the catastrophe of Asia Minor, whose coasts had been trodden by Homer, Heraclitus of Ephesus, and Thales of Miletus—the philosopher who diverted the course of the River Halys so Croesus's army could cross into Cappadocia to confront Cyrus the Great.

Turkish peasants in turbans, with curved daggers, were sitting in a café playing trictrac, not far from a camel encampment, and with a black dog stretched out among them.

Drunken soldiers had overturned stones and crosses along

the paths of the Greek cemetery, east of the Aydin rail station. The gravestones, bearing the names of the deceased and the dates of their short span on Earth, had not escaped the nocturnal vandals and were splashed with raki. In the midday glare many names foundered in an ocean of light.

Past the stony tumuli of the *koimeterion*, the cemetery where the dead would sleep until the Day of Resurrection, in whose open graves many Greeks now hid their daughters from the Turks or themselves from the *chettes*, Nicias descended into the secret hypogeum, the underground chamber that housed the Andrakis family mausoleum.

On the main wall of the first space gleamed a mosaic of Christ Pantocrator, holding a book. The gold of the letters Alpha and Omega lit up the penumbra. Opposite there was an image of the Genethlia Theotokou—the birth of the mother of God—and a statue of the Virgin Mary seated on a throne of charred wood, in a magus's robe and with a baby Jesus on her knee.

In the second space Nicias saw a Phoenix rearing between motionless flames, a symbol of resurrection. Then he entered the small cubicle, or "place of slumber," a common euphemism for such repositories of corpses.

On the tomb of Eurydice Andrakis, his Smyrnean cousin, his fiancée until the day he enlisted in the Greek army, he was shaken to see her likeness carved in low relief. At first he did not recognize her and believed it must be someone else, for he could not imagine her to be dead. Then he looked again and saw that it resembled the girl whose photograph had gone with him to the war. In that picture she stood at the center of a rosette formed by her schoolmates, dressed in white robes and diadems. All the girls were smiling cheerfully at the camera.

The sight of the carving plunged Nicias painfully into the past. He remembered the summers they had spent together on the Aegean coast, and relived with especial longing that evening stroll through St. Anne's Valley, eating figs and chocolates, when both were studying in Greek schools: she at the Omereion School for Girls, and he at the Evangelical School of Smyrna. Nobody who had seen them that day could ever have forgotten their eyes ablaze with dreams, the dreams of a world that yielded up its wonders at every instant. Since then he had not lain with any woman; his only lover had been solitude.

"Why have you abandoned Helios to enter this sorrowful place?" he imagined her asking.

"I came here because Calliope told me to," he answered himself.

She said no more. Her psyche retained no imprint of itself, although he still cherished physical recollections of her, as in the Cavafy poem where the body's memory rekindles an old yearning in the blood; the memory of the sensual pleasures of lips and skin and hands, which no sooner evoked are experienced afresh.

"There is an Orpheus inside each one of us, but I want to see her alive," Nicias said. To him the figure in the relief was not his girlfriend, merely a glimpse reflected in a watery mirror, in a dream.

Leaving the hypogeum, he came upon a chapel with arches and apses, bearing an inscription in Greek:

O CHRIST PANTOCRATOR, CREATOR OF ALL THINGS
AND ALL MEN,
TAKE UNDER YOUR PROTECTION PENELOPE,
THEOLOGOS,
KOSTAS AND HERMIONE, NICIAS AND EURYDICE.
PRAYER UPON THE PASSING OF SWEET EURYDICE
ANDRAKIS, FOREVER IN OUR HEARTS.

Nicias read the dates of her birth and death: Mytilene, 1900–
Smyrna, 1919. "She died only months after the Greeks disembarked in Smyrna," he thought, although he felt convinced that she was not in her tomb. A letter wrapped around a stone, written in blue ink, confirmed it: "Eurydice is alive. Look for her in the Jewish cemetery. Burn this message. C."

The cemetery paths were littered with crosses torn from their headstones. Some he lifted up, others he left. He walked through a field of asphodels. The gray spectral meadow suited the bleakness of his mood, and when he heard a cry in a tree he thought of the owl of the Greek goddess. But it was not Athena's bird; it was a bat.

In this crepuscule that might be dawn or dusk, he found it apt to compare the armies of shades gathered on the banks of the Acheron with the Greek soldiers trailing around Smyrna's quays. The autumn asphodels with their brittle stalks, unpleasant smell, and tangled foliage like fallen hair not only represented the sustenance of disembodied spirits in the place of their "repose," but the very image of the refugees.

"If children of the gods and heroes slain in battle go to the Elysian Fields, where will the Greeks murdered in Smyrna be received?" Nicias wondered. He saw a black-robed, white-bearded monk in the meadow, with a crown of woven grasses on his head, picking different species of asphodels—*albus*, *cerasiferus*, *ramosus*, and *aestivus*. Among the blooms lay men and women feigning death.

The monk walked away. Nicias remembered that this plant also thrives in the underworld, and its flowers are regarded as favorites of the dead. This is why it was said in Smyrna that Odysseus waited for the deceased among the asphodels. While at this very moment ghoulish Charon might be conducting a legion of ghosts to the Elysian Fields or to Hades, the abode of the "Unseen," there were also middling souls, with no allotted fate, hovering amongst the plants as if in a vegetal labyrinth, not knowing that in the here and now the other world gives signs of life by way of asphodels.

On his way to the Jewish quarter, whose steep streets afforded a magnificent view over the bay, Nicias passed the oft-burned and rebuilt church of Agios Ioannis Theologos before reaching the Jewish cemetery to seek Eurydice. A woman's voice was singing in Ladino:

As trees weep for the rains, as mountains weep for breezes, so mine eyes do weep for thee, dear love. To alien lands I go, I go to die. Before me stands an angel, with his eyes he looks on me. Fain would I weep and I cannot. My heart breaks in a sigh, I turn and say to thee: What will become of me? To alien lands I go, I go to die.

Thinking it might be Eurydice singing the old lament which the Sephardi took with them on leaving Spain in 1492, he hunted for her among funerary slabs incised with Stars of David and menorahs. But she was nowhere to be found. The singer too had vanished into thin air.

"Here is the key to my house in the Kal of Kastiya." Finally, at the gates, an old woman came to meet him. Hoping for some message from Eurydice, he waited as she drew near. But when she stretched out her hand to give him something, she murmured words about the key to her ancestral home in Castile.

Instead of a key, she pressed into his palm a poem on a scrap of paper: "Zacuto is thinking of Zacuta." It was dedicated to Penelope de Juan (the name of Nicias's mother), written in Ladino by one Juan Martines, and the last line enjoined: "Seek her tonight at Chez Friné. Burn this message. C."

Hungry for life, and even more for the city, Nicias went through the Frank quarter to the bazaar district and the main square, then from the city prison to the Ephesian gates, and from the Turkish cemeteries known as Namaziak (near the agora of Smyrna) and Moussala. He crossed the Caravan Bridge, on the far side of which stood the marble lion that had fascinated him since adolescence; walked along the railway tracks of the Aydin and Cassaba lines, whose lucrative construction had pitted the British against the French; and entered St. Anne's Valley, passing by the old Kamares Aqueduct on the road to Boudja.

In the station he discovered a freight train with a car full of ears poking through the bars. A woeful braying suggested that a female was being mounted by a male. They were wild asses from Cappadocia, "land of beautiful horses" and, he thought, of beautiful donkeys, too.

Roped by Turkish peasants in caves and gullies, the "lunar landscape" of Central Anatolia, the animals were to be transported to Smyrna on the Ottoman Railway Company line. Nicias recalled as he looked at them how Greek soldiers often took refuge in the Anatolian underground cities of Kaymakli and Derinkuyu, where some levels still had ventilation shafts and wells.

It was then he saw a man in a black suit and hat slipping his right hand into a crack in a tree trunk. Withdrawing a piece of paper, he appeared to set off towards Agios Ioannis Prodromos, in Cordelio. But he was not really going to the church, because minutes later he reappeared at the station from another direction, this time carrying a black suitcase.

The man halted in front of a passenger car that had been decoupled from the others and was stationed by the water mill that supplied the locomotives. He found that the passengers were refugees, the doors were locked, and nobody was allowed on or off. Clustered around the windows, women and children craned their necks for a glimpse of the platforms, the drab countryside around the station, the cypresses and pine trees, and the three wisps of white cloud. From inside the car came the sound of murmurs and movements, the voices of hundreds of people who seemed to be enclosed in a human hive. Outside the train a black-clad woman was sitting on the stony ground, with black hair and a black parasol, like an inert shadow, a dark blot gazing at the car in expectation of the arrival of the driver or conductor. Then Nicias noticed the man in black laboring down the platform with his heavy case. Up close, he thought he recognized Professor Seferiades. But it was not Seferiades, it was somebody very like him. After half an hour, the most frustrating thing for the man and the travelers trapped inside the closed car was to realize that this train would leave neither that day nor the next, since all passenger schedules and ticket sales had been suspended by the Turkish military government.

After the freight train with its cargo of asses pulled out of the station towards Smyrna, the man in black began to pace up and down the platform, plainly agitated, not to say desperate. At last he sat down on a stone, opened the black suitcase and starting flinging books and clothing onto the tracks.

Nicias sensed that this man had finally given up the wait for some companion, his wife, perhaps, or his daughter: she had been arrested by the Turks and would never arrive.

There was a great deal of activity in the port around the ships moored to the quays, as goods were loaded and unloaded. Nicias witnessed a working day on Smyrna's docks, grooved by train tracks and bustling with carts and wagons. Opposite were rows of storefronts shaded by awnings, and maritime offices with employees and clients coming out. The main post office, where he dropped a letter to his brother Niarchos in Brussels, was an imposing building that had previously housed the National Bank of Greece, and earlier still, the Bourse.

A caravan of camels laden with sacks of figs was moving past the Banco di Roma. Blinkered piebald horses drew streetcars, carriages, and wagons, casting warm shadows. Parked up by the quays were the Packards, Oldsmobiles, and Fords recently purchased by the Levantine owners of the large corporations operating in Smyrna. Barges heaped with sacks of grain rocked gently on the water.

Nicias took an internal staircase through the Sporting Club to gain the terrace. From its mirador he contemplated the bay, the ships, the mountains, the Point, the white villas of Bella Vista, the camels kneeling on the pier. It was hot, and Café Costi and the Grand Hotel Kraemer Palace were busy. A streetcar jangled past behind its horse.

Nicias left the Sporting Club, the porters scowling at his attire. He crossed the hotel passage. In Frank Street he glanced into the Au Bon Marché department store and the opticians Perera Frères, and looked from the sidewalk at the window displays of the specialized importers of European goods, the Anglo-Eastern Cooperative, Solari and Xenopolu & Co., and those of the confectionery boutiques with their boxes of bonbons, pralines, and chocolate bars from Mexico, Holland, Switzerland, and Italy such as Johfrej, De Gruyters, Lindt, Suchard, Caffarel, and Toblerone. He walked past the Oriental Carpet Manufacturers, the Banque d'Orient, the Icard Pharmacy, and the Great Britain Pharmacy, in the knowledge that he couldn't afford rugs or medicines, he couldn't deposit or withdraw money, or even buy some lotion for his dry hands. Standing in front of the seafood restaurants he had the sense that he, like the squid, belonged to another life. And at the little stalls selling thyme honey, walnuts, and hazelnuts, he felt fiercely frustrated: these delicacies laid out before his eyes were beyond his reach.

He considered exchanging the two or three crumpled bills in

his pocket for a much-needed bath at Pangalos, in the Rue Par-
allèle, near the French Consulate, then changed his mind,
deciding to spend the little he had left on food.

He dropped into the Sporting Club again, where the regattas
used to begin. None of the regattas that made for the Point—
for Europeans, for local people, for fishermen—had ever inter-
ested him. Traditionally, the competition had been enlivened
by two orchestras, the municipal band and the Greek orphanage band. Up on the terrace, Nicias thought back to the club's
balconies in the days when they were crowded with cheering
Greeks, Turks, Jews, Armenians, and Levantines, like the picture of a lost world. And in the same moment he viewed the
vessels rocking on the waters of the Gulf of Smyrna just as if
his own dead body were floating there on the dark waves.

Like a premonition of what was soon to unfold, he saw Turkish secret agents on the stone balconies of the Banque d'Athènes
spying on the Greeks on the shopping street. They were doubt-
less watching him too, because one of them dropped his eyes
when he looked at him, and shortly afterward appeared slink-
ing along the street, hugging the wall. Aware of being a wanted
man, Nicias tried to get away, only to see the agent relayed by a
goat-faced, shifty-eyed *chette*, bandoleers crossed over his chest
and a sheathed dagger at his belt.

He evaded that *chette* but another promptly showed up,
scrawny and unkempt, with a lopsided mouth and dirty hands.
He dodged that one by merging with a flock of ragged refugees, useful for concealment. Then he stepped into a house with
tumbledown walls and shattered windows as though he lived

there, and slipped out into a back alley. He had escaped for now, but he knew he would meet his pursuer again.

After sundown, the hour when the blue begins to darken and the contours of houses grow blurred, Nicias climbed to the top of Mount Pagus, around which the city of Smyrna was founded: "jewel of Asia," "city of life," "capital of tolerance."

Here, in ancient times, Nemesis was worshipped and Saint Polycarp was burned alive. From the fortress Nicias gazed at the city and its port: the old military and commercial harbors, the vestiges of archaic, Hellenistic, and Roman Smyrna; the Caravan Bridge; the gateways to Ephesus and Magnesia; the library and the Omereion; and Homer's Meles River, which once lapped the foot of the walls and flowed out into the bay. He thought of the legend of Smyrna, which Pausanias relates, telling how Alexander the Great, resting under a plane tree from a day's hunting on these very slopes, was visited in a dream by Nemesis, who commanded him to rebuild the city. He recalled that, according to Strabo, though the city had been refounded by Antigonus, it was Lysimachus who rebuilt it, and named it Eurydiceia in honor of his daughter Eurydice.

Nicias looked out towards the faraway Point. His gaze swept the gas works and Bournabat Bay, the Smyrnaia Textiles Co-Partnership buildings, the Anglo-Eastern Cooperative Co. office, the Anglican church and the French hospital, and the whitewashed, red-tiled dwellings of the Greek and Armenian districts. He contemplated the Cassaba and Aydin train lines, and sought for the remains of the vast theater that Vitruvius mentions. In Bayrakli he made out the church of the Capuchin friars, not far from the railway, and the ruins of the Temple of Athena.

The ancient landscape was alive with flowers. Scattered boulders kept company with broken statues, and black, parched, stunted pine trees guarded the dead beneath their dappled shade. The landscape seemed both different and the same, like the sea; its alterations were barely noticeable: a few pebbles and grasses, a few buried shadows come back to life, stirred by the breeze.

"He's watching me," thought Nicias: he had just noticed the scrawny, slovenly agent behind a pine tree. "Am I a danger to the Ottoman Empire? Am I going to be arrested, assassinated?" The spy's eyes were green, yellow, coal-black, camouflaged by the lowering dusk.

"Better return to the port." By descending to the city, he hoped to avoid any undesirable encounters. As he walked past the spy, he caught a sidelong glimpse of the headline in the newspaper he was reading:

THE GREEKS ARE RAPING OUR WOMEN. THE
GREEKS ARE BURNING OUR CITIES.
DEATH TO THE GREEKS!

Which paper was it? *L'Impérial*, *Le Levant*, the *Journal de Smyrne*? A Turkish paper?

At the foot of the hill, he came upon a seated man with a face like tree bark. It was Alexis. A native of Chios, he had wanted to see the world and signed up on a ship bound for San Diego.

In his student days, Nicias used to come across him on the docks with a Cappadocian turtle on a leash, its shell so black that it seemed capped by a flake of night. Other times he was cradling an angora cat, or a laughing owl he'd brought back from New Zealand, whose chuckle was so melancholy that its last notes sounded eaten up by twilight. When it laughed, the shrill sound climaxed in a shout. Afterward the bird would sink into profound lethargy, until its eyes flew open. Its body snuggled in a blanket of feathers.

"Hello, Nicias, hello, Nicias," the old sailor greeted him, like a parrot.

In the fig market the vendors had opened their sacks for customers to buy small or bulk quantities of the fruit brought by caravans of camels from the interior to Smyrna. Lighters stood by, ready to convey the harvest to the islands.

Nicias observed the small signs of everyday market life: a blue-painted ladder propped against a wall, a white cross hung from rafters like a puppet, a man trying to make out the shape of a Levantine girl through her thick wads of clothing, a pair of traders conversing with their backs to a photographer who was taking pictures of the figs.

"*Marché aux figues,*" "*Feigenmarkt im Bazar,*" the foreigners could be heard saying, while young Greek matrons squatted beside their baskets to select the best of the recent crop. Others stood and pointed to the fruits packed in boxes on the ground. Out in the street white-veiled Turkish girls peddled the most damaged fruit to unfussy housewives, ignoring the camels plodding by with sacks of figs from the orchards of J. Christidi.

This cargo hailed from plantations in Inovassi Erbeily, the best and most fertile in Asia Minor, and was headed for the Deirmendjiek Station to be exported.

Nicias was enjoying the sight of the local beauties gathered at a long table to sample the figs; he was particularly taken with one rustic Aphrodite—her white blouse garlanded by a string of figs like red-white roses on her breast, her mischievous smile, fig in hand—when Turkish soldiers burst in, kicking baskets and squashing figs under their boots as if they were human eyes. No, the irruption of the troops was not part of Smyrna's fig festival, when men and women danced on the railway tracks among camels and musicians; it was a more serious matter: they were taking control of the market.

Before the scattered fruits of that tree of milky, bitter sap, summoned forth from the Athenian earth by the goddess Demeter, he felt wounded by the profanation, as if it were the nadir of the miseries of the age. He remembered that Plato was nicknamed *"filosikos,"* fig-lover, and how it was the exquisite savor of its figs that moved Xerxes to conquer Attica, and how he himself, as a child, used to run through the orchards of Tire gathering the white figs of Smyrna with his father.

Theologos and Penelope, his parents, had lived in Athens until 1908, when they bought land in Asia Minor to grow tobacco and vines, but the first thing they planted was fig trees.

Their four sons and two daughters tended the orchards on the outskirts of Tire, and they had a tailor's shop and a clothing store in the center of town. But not a day passed without showing reverence to the goddess Demeter, and they planted as many fig trees as possible in the garden of their home. The

Turkish laborers, on meeting his father, would kiss his hand. Nicias attended primary school in the mornings and helped out with the trees in the afternoons.

Theologos made few improvements to his property; he didn't paint the walls of the house, or buy furniture, or give Penelope new clothes; all he did was add more fig trees. He spent his time in the orchards observing how they grew and how the fruits changed color, and whether their flesh was white or red and their skins green, black, or violet. Of his acquaintances he liked to say, "They only come to see me when the figs are ripe."

When the time came for high school, Nicias went to Smyrna, a hundred kilometers from Tire, and it was from his Greek teachers that he heard tell for the first time of the Megali Idea. When the Great War broke out, and the Turks allied with the Germans, and British warships and planes shelled the port, the train stations, and the Turkish quarter, he hastened to enlist in the Greek army and was sent to the island of Samos. From there he was dispatched with a garrison to Kavala, near the Greco-Bulgarian border, to guard a bridge.

After the defeat of the Greek army and the slaughter of the people of Asia Minor by the Turks, and before gaining Smyrna, Nicias went first to Tire, to look for his parents.

Crossing the hostile town, he approached his old home. The gate lock was rusty. He put a hand through a gap in the metal to open it. The iron's groan startled him, as though the past itself were speaking. As he pushed the gate ajar, it squealed chillingly. To walk through the small fig grove was like trampling over generations of people and leaves splayed like hands.

Only shoddy repairs had been carried out during his absence. A nude statue of Tiresias adorned the fountain, which had been filled in. The withered penis, in a bag with four testicles like empty grape-skins, testified to an audacious taste. A ladder leaning on a wall seemed to have been placed there by his father to seek the evening, but it was only two meters high. Suddenly he felt observed from a window. The four eyes of a marble owl, a bifronted Athena, were fixed on him.

The packets of flour and bags of raisins and dried figs in the pantry suggested that his parents had departed in a hurry. And yet some dishes had recently been washed. The old furniture in the living and dining rooms, which they hadn't managed to sell, gave him the poignant sensation of a childhood that had not only aged, but had been disdained as commercially worthless.

Standing in his former bedroom he felt like an exile, a missing person in his own home, and he imagined the diaspora that awaited him. A photograph of himself, aged twelve, forgotten in a drawer, demoralized him. But the most upsetting moment came when he noticed the dereliction of the fig tree outside his window—his fig tree: a metaphor for his life.

He was ready to leave when he heard footsteps in the hall. Thinking his father had returned, he went to the door. It was the old Turkish servant who had instilled bad habits in him since boyhood. She appeared like a specter from the past, a specter come to haunt him with memories. He made to shoo her away. But the old crone was stubborn, and her hands were full of honey cakes. The presence of honey (his last name meant "honey maker" in Greek) disarmed him, and he ended up embracing her. Upon which she launched into a babble of people and places, trying to express that his parents and siblings had left Tire: "Theologos, Penelope, Volos, Volos, Volos, Theologos, Penelope, Volos, Volos; Cleomenis, Niarchos, Utrecht, Brussels, Utrecht, Brussels." After a pause, even though he hadn't asked about the other Greeks who had left town, she loosed a cascade of classical names borne by everyday folks: "Homer, Thales, Aphrodite, Philoctetes, Aeschylus, Herodotus, Hermione, Antigone, Artemis, Plato, Pericles."

As he walked out of the house, Nicias became aware of a little Turkish girl staring at him from behind the door. She had the archaic Greek smile on her face.

Wednesday, September 6. Roving aimlessly in Smyrna among the destitute and the defeated, Nicias was reminded of the loneliness that had paralyzed him throughout the glacial wartime nights as he was guarding the frontier bridge—that miserable bridge nobody ever used, from whence not a living soul could be found for miles.

He rehearsed the facts that irked him like a fishbone stuck in the throat: in anticipation of the Treaty of Sèvres, which granted to Greece the mandate over Smyrna and Eastern Thrace, and supported by one British and two Greek destroyers plus the battleship *Kilkis*, Greek troops had disembarked in the city's port on May 15, 1919, and since then the clashes with the Turks had grown more bitter.

The day of the landing, he and thousands of fellow soldiers were welcomed with festive joy by a multitude of Greek and Armenian civilians, and blessed by Archbishop Chrysostomos; he had experienced a fleeting sense of victory then. But all too soon, dragged into a mercilessly cruel war, he found himself billeted with four hundred others on the shores of the Marmara Sea. Camped on a mountain one moonless night, believing they heard regiments of Turks climbing up the forest tracks towards them, they fired frantically into the darkness. At daybreak they found twenty-five dead boars among the trees.

Months later, as Greek forces pushed deeper into Turkey, he got a sight of Ankara through his field glasses. The Greek advance was unstoppable. But Eleftherios Venizelos had the bright idea to hold a general election in Greece, and the army was called back to oversee the polling process in Thebes and Thessaly. By the time the soldiers returned to Asia Minor the Turks had regrouped, and fought back ferociously. All this filled Nicias's mind as he made his way to the main square. But on seeing a detachment of Turkish soldiers heading to their barracks along the Quay, he knew that they would double back from another side, taking the refugees by surprise, and so he took the opposite direction.

It was an ideal sunny evening for enjoying Smyrna. Greek girls in white frocks with colorful sunshades strolled down Frank Street, escorted by black-clad men wearing boaters or felt hats. The refugees trailed through the waterfront restaurant and hotel zone with long faces, as if the affluence of others made their lot harder to bear. Foreigners in their own land, to which the Turks now laid claim, women from the Greek and Armenian quarters were anxiously pacing the quays with their children, determined to get out on the first boat that would take them or the first train to leave the Smyrna Cassaba Railway station. Meanwhile, Greek soldiers in civilian clothes arriving from Asia Minor were contemplating the French pier, by the

Point, as if the sloops moored in front of the offices dealing with passports and health permits were so many optical illusions. A streetcar trundled by, pulled by a blinkered white horse. Mount Pagus loomed up over the city. Facing out to sea, the white hulk of the Oriental Carpet Manufacturers warehouse dominated the view.

"*Souvenir de Smyrne*" was the caption on the postcard Nicias was about to send to his parents—a panoramic photograph of the city taken from the sea—when he heard a man coughing, seated at a café table. His jacket was creased and his expression betrayed a splitting headache. Undistracted by the throng, he was reading a newspaper article:

THE MEGALI IDEA IS DEAD

The Megali Idea, proclaimed in 1844 by Ioannis Kolettis, is dead. . . . But it may yet resurrect. On the scale of world history, 1922 is nothing but a speck in time. The Greek gods still exist, and Poseidon may one day unleash an earthquake. Let us not forget: "The Kingdom of Greece is not Greece. It constitutes only one part, the smallest and feeblest. The name Hellenes describes not only those who live in this kingdom, but also those who live in Jannina, in Thessaloniki, in Serres, in Adrianople, in Constantinople, in Trebizond, in Crete, in Samos and in any territory associated with Hellenic history and the Hellenic race."[2]

---

[2] Ioannis Kolettis, *Discourses of Collective Identity in Central and Southeast Europe (1770–1945): Texts and Commentaries, vol. 2, National Romanticism: The Formation of National Movements*, ed. Michal Kopeček and Balázs Trencsényi, trans. Mary Kitroeff (Budapest: Central European University Press, 2007), 248.

Behind the round spectacles and snowy hair, Nicias recognized his old high school teacher. But he couldn't remember his name; his memory had been split in two by the war. This man conveyed a solitude that was existential as well as physical. He was spearing Syrian dates with a fork, so that his fingers wouldn't get sticky as he read an item about the execution of Henri Désiré Landru, convicted of murdering ten women and guillotined in the Versailles prison on February 25 of that year. Soon he forgot about Landru and stared down at his chair, as if to divine not only his own fate but also the stabbings of the hours to come.

"Who is Constantine Cavafy? An exile from his time? An Alexandrian poet who died a thousand years ago, to be buried by the Turks in the dungeon of history? Who is Cavafy?" the man said to Nicias. At the sound of his voice, the name came back to him: Alexis Seferiades, whom he thought he had seen the other day at the train station.

When on the afternoon of September 7, Georgios Hatzianestis—the general with legs of glass—rose from his bed, he did so not to plan the counter-offensive against the Turks, but to abandon Smyrna. After all, he had been relieved of his command before the decisive defeats.

Standing up, he slapped his calves with both hands to make sure his lower limbs could withstand the journey in one piece. He donned his military regalia, as if preparing for a parade. He lifted a corner of the rug and pried a small box of gold coins from under a floorboard, then cleared all his papers out of the drawers—it was too risky to carry them on his person—and he asked an aide to take them in a document case. After checking that his pistol was loaded, he stepped into the street. The crowd in the harbor jeered and booed, especially when he was seen mounting the gangway of a transport ship. Impervious to their insults, he stood on the bridge issuing orders to the crew as the vessel steamed away over the horizon.

Aristides Stergiades, the Greek high commissioner of Smyrna, was observed boarding the ship, where he signed over the Greek orphanage at Boudja to the American International College, perhaps his last official act. No word came from the local authorities, or the Greek fleet, or the gendarmes who were so fond of being snapped in heroic poses in front of their barracks and school. Such desertions infuriated the crowd, and people began shouting loudly in protest. Although M. Graillet, the French consul-general in Smyrna, who had been given the keys to the Konak—the city's seat of government—by Stergiades, attempted to maintain public order and safety, the city was effectively rudderless until Turkish troops took control by deploying mounted patrols and infantry squads. In the meantime, George Horton watched from the terrace of the American consulate as dozens of panic-stricken refugees, mostly Greek women with infants in their arms, sought refuge and sanctuary in the consulate grounds.

The Christian population, reduced to the same helpless condition as the refugees, flocked to the railway station. But the Muslims fired at the Greek soldiers who were overseeing the departure of the train, shot a couple of citizens in rags, and threw a uniformed soldier into the sea, hands bound and with a sandbag tied to his back.

Eddying up and down the winding Frank Street was a throng of women, called Iphigenia, Electra, Helene, Calliope, Antigone, Evangelia, Aphrodite, Sappho, Hermione, and Maria. They mixed with men named Alexis, Aristides, Alcibiades, Philoctetes, Petros, Evangelos, Apostolos, Kyrillos, Aristoteles, Anatolios, Sergios, Pericles, Solon, Aristophanes, Perseus, or Minos. Some entered shops at random, others made for the bazaar and the main harbor road, and a few aimed for the Levantine quarter in Bournabat, not because they hailed from there, but to beg food or shelter from the residents.

Nicias managed to get on a steam train to Paradise, the "little corner of America," so called for its gardens, brand new buildings, and professorial homes equipped with running water. In his worn boots and decaying socks, his pockets empty, he walked slowly in the vicinity of the American International College, scanning the facades for the American, French, or Italian flags that might signal sanctuary. The suburb's streets were deserted, now that Turkish soldiers were shooting right, left, and center, and the carriageway had turned into a morass of war junk; it was littered with broken rifles, orphaned jackets, military uniforms, shoes full of holes, trampled portraits, cracked spectacles, blood-stained bandages, and useless cannon and vehicles. The discarded garments would have served to clothe the invisible man, for many soldiers had removed their uniforms in an attempt to rid them of any vestiges of living men. From time to time the warbling of a lone bird followed Nicias, like a sweet foretaste of fall.

"Catch that Greek soldier. Get him, kill him!" The door of an army jeep opened behind him and a thin, grimy officer began shooting. The bullets smashed into pebbles and weeds around him as he threw himself face down. Leaving him for dead, the officer got back into his jeep to chase a Greek girl walking by the side of the road. An old man lifted Nicias up and led him into a tavern full of jittery customers downing cheap wine. The news of Nikolaos Trikoupis's capture by the Turks spurred the Greek soldiers to tear off their uniforms and get into civvies. The change of clothes made them disappear. But it was not enough to save them, for their physical appearance gave them away. The local snitches denounced them. Their neighbors, wielding guns and knives and dressed as enemies, poisoned their water, put ground glass into their food, shot them in the back. Man: an unknown.

"Where did September the eighth go?" wondered Nicias to himself, amid disturbing rumors that the war was coming to Smyrna and that Afyon, Magnesia, and other cities of Asia Minor were ablaze already. As these reports came in, the British authorities were discussing whether to send troops to Bournabat to guard the property of their nationals, provided it could be done without appearing like a provocation to Turkish troops; the American high commissioner, Admiral Bristol, was expressing full confidence in the Ottomans' good intentions—their administration of Smyrna would be benevolent, in his opinion—and the Greek newspapers were insisting that their army's retreat was purely tactical, that there were plans to defend the city, and that its inhabitants were not in danger from the Turks. Such were the claims; but Consul Horton received a visit from the Greek metropolitan Chrysostomos, and when they were alone in his office he urged the prelate to flee the city, for he recognized the shadow of impending death upon his face.

Saturday, September 9. An ashen sun gleamed in the sky like a moldy apple. The mirage of a city at peace was breaking up, and every opportunity for pillage was pounced on. Finding them unguarded, the locals looted the Greek army storehouses. Horse-drawn wagons packed with barrels of cooking oil, sacks of flour, and cartons of sugar were led through the streets by men, women, and children who reckoned that these goods were better off taken by them than by the Turks.

Gangs of *chettes*, the thieving, criminal swine used by the Turkish army as irregulars, materialized in public spaces and shopping streets. People were convinced that some had been there since May 1919, the date of the Greek landing, and more had been steadily infiltrating the city thereafter. Descriptions of their physical traits were frequent preludes to tales of atrocity and murder.

"The barbarians have arrived. They were expected in three days' time, but they came today," said Seferiades, the white-haired man with round spectacles he had seen in the café, to Nicias. At school this man had told him about Constantine Cavafy, the poet he encountered in Athens in 1905, both having been to the Hermes School of Commerce in Alexandria, after which they had kept in touch through postcards. Seferiades had sent Cavafy one captioned "*Marché aux figues dans les bazars*," dated Smyrna, September 29, 1911. The last message he received from Cavafy in Alexandria was a poem, "The God Abandons Antony."

"What do you mean?"

"The barbarians have arrived."

"The Turks entered the city. They came from the south, burning villages and towns. The girls at the college saw them go by as they were doing calisthenics in the schoolyard. They turned their heads to look at the *chettes*. The *chettes* all fixed leering gazes upon the Levantine maidens with arms aloft in their black-and-white blouses and long skirts over laced boo-tees. Bournabat had fled. The houses were in darkness. Five thousand *chettes* arrived bent on killing, plunder, and rape."

The man peered short-sightedly at Nicias, studying his reac-tion. "Have we met before? Where?"

"At school."

"I know you met Professor Seferiades, but I don't know whether Professor Seferiades met you."

The sound of trotting horses could be heard. Turkish troops were entering the city. Greeks and Armenians ran to conceal themselves in homes and stores.

"Don't pretend you don't know; pack your belongings and bid Smyrna farewell, for Smyrna has betrayed you. My own escape will be through the grand front door of death."

With these words Alexis Seferiades climbed onto a block of stone. White hair ruffled by the breeze, eyes bright behind thick lenses, he gazed into the distance, listening to the sea. He began to recite: "When they saw Patroclus dead, the horses of Achilles began to weep; their immortal nature was upset deeply by this work of death they had to look at." Then he stepped down, and walked away from the Turks.

How far would he get? Where had he come from and where was he going? Where had he got hold of that green velvet jacket? Nicias watched him move off down the narrow street, uncertain whether his presence was real or an aural hallucination. As the other turned the corner he recalled that Seferiades had been the first, on the subject of the "incantation of light," to tell his class about *The Student of Prague*—that film in which a young man disposed to magic duels to the death with his mirror double.

The Turkish cavalry was riding down the harbor road, having secured the docks with emplacements of cannon and other ordnance, while the side streets were blocked by infantry platoons.

This was the formal entrance into Smyrna of Mustafa Kemal's troops. The mounted regiment, all in black, their inky fezzes displaying a red crescent and red star, advanced among banners and scimitars. Battle-hardened foot soldiers with Mongolian features marched with a disdainful air, looking neither right nor left, towards the Konak, where they would hoist the national flag at the top of the main building.

The Turkish population welcomed their army by decorating shop windows, house-fronts, trees, and lampposts with pieces of red fabric. The ponderous strains of patriotic music rang out from the balconies, and women holding armfuls of flowers came over the water on launches. In the main square, around the monumental clock tower and its four fountains, men waved red flags and brandished sabers, rifles, and portraits of Kemal as though to defy the Greek and Armenian inhabitants. Some cavalrymen called out to the terrified people, "Don't be afraid, don't be afraid!"

Among the onlookers at this parade of Kemalist troops under General Murcelle Pasha were Levantines from Bournabat, Boudja, Cordelio, and Paradise, mixed with many Armenians and Greeks, men and women who stared in bafflement at such a ferocious show of strength.

"I believe I've seen the fellow before," said an Englishman who was in Smyrna to buy carpets.

"Who?" an American schoolteacher inquired.

"Murcelle Pasha. The other night I came across him in a sodomite establishment—one that escaped being closed by Stergiades because it's run by foreigners—dressed as a woman; but don't tell a soul. To see the wrong person in the wrong place can be fatal."

The rejoicing continued until an unseen hand lobbed a grenade in front of the Passport Office, causing superficial face wounds to a Turkish officer. That was the pretext for the Kemalist troops stationed in front of the railings that protected the Konak to march into the Armenian quarter and begin the killing.

It might have seemed a simple matter for the Turks to overrun this neighborhood, but the area was a densely populated warren of small streets and whitewashed, red-roofed houses. Grande Rue Armenienne Resadiye, Rue Russan, Grand Rue Basmahane, Rue Vemian, Rue Ste.-Paraskevi, Rue Sahin, Grand Rue Fethiye, Rue Moda, Grand Rue Meles, Grand Rue Kemer, Rue Suzan, Rue Derder, Rue Kabouroglou. Streets that linked churches, hospitals, schools for boys or girls, railway stations, and big mansions such as that of Dr. Garabed Hatcherian and those of the Aram, Berberian, Atamian, Kasparian, Hartunian, Balikjian, and Arakelian families; here too lived Hovekim Uregian, who had angled a mirror in his corner window so as to observe from within the house the "inferno of blood" and "small girls being defiled in the street by the Turks."

The bands of irregulars, with their crossed bullet belts and fistfuls of rifles, garrotes, and daggers, were breaking into shops and homes to commit pillage, murder, and havoc. Their appearance heralded violence and death. Earlier Nicias had seen them go by in gangs of twenty or thirty, in the direction of the city center and towards the villas of Cordelio, Boudja, Bournabat, and Paradise.

"What's going on next door?" he heard an Armenian woman say, leaning out of a window.

"Probably a cat trying to get out," her husband replied from the darkened room beyond.

"It's not an animal; it's a man with blood on his hands. I'm afraid for the children we left alone in the house," the woman said. When she went into the street she was stopped by a gaggle of *chettes* who began to surround her, pointing, pawing, lifting her clothing, some roaring with laughter, others smoking hashish.

"Let me pass!" She struggled to fight them off with mounting terror.

"Where shall we take her? To the Konak or the Armenian cemetery?" joked one, and his gun's loud reports made the Armenian woman clap her hands over her ears.

"Leave not a single one alive; grind them into the ground; nobody will obstruct our road to victory!" The words slid out sideways through the crooked mouth of a bandit with a sharp snout and yellow eyes; his neck, poking up above the white cloths covering his chest and shoulders, appeared deformed.

Women and children could be heard screaming inside a house. The cries were first piercing, then faint. A smell of grime, dead meat, and blood-soaked clothing rose from a broken drain.

Hiding in every room were women, old people, children, and men who had survived deportation by the Ottomans to Changra. The sick, the dying, and the dead had been left to rot on the floor. Others watched the movements of a *chette* recklessly engaged in plunder and rape. Nicias got a glimpse of his hands on the breasts of a little girl. Like a louse he explored her nakedness, slid over her body, bit her, pinched her, pecked her. Dishes and flower vases went crashing. Her father who came between them was stabbed with a knife.

The little girl rushed out of a back door. Beside herself with fear, she clung to Nicias's knees. In a mixture of Armenian and Greek she begged him to save her. But the *chette* dragged her back indoors, threw her face down on the rug and penetrated her like a dog. Her younger brother, hiding in the adjoining room, scratching on the windowpane, watched the deflowering.

The Turkish soldiers cordoned off the Armenian quarter. The inhabitants were no longer safe behind their own front doors. Families locked down in their homes began to feel helpless and forsaken. Outside, bands of *chettes* communicated by means of blood-curdling squeals.

The stores pulled down their shutters. The theft of flour, oil, sugar, and other staples had become commonplace. Food was growing scarce. Turkish soldiers broke down the doors of ostensibly deserted houses with their rifle-butts to commit robbery, rape, and murder. When the neighbors realized what was going on, they grew panic-stricken; afterward they crept fearfully towards the scene of the crimes, and as fearfully backed away once they learned the facts.

In Frank Street the *chettes* were stealing jewelry, rugs, cash, fine clothes, chocolates, wine, household goods, and anything else of value. In a service area at the back of a store, Nicias saw the irregulars tip a pan of scalding lentil soup into the lap of a cook, who ran out into the street squealing with pain; but at the sight of another bunch of bandits, she fled back in again.

"In the suburb of Boudja, the cavalry killed Oscar and Cleo de Jongh. For lack of caskets the Dutch couple's bodies could not be buried and were left beneath a tree, among other trees where abused Armenian girls had been suspended naked from the branches, some by their belts, others by their hair." This was the last news Nicias heard that night.

Sunday, September 10. In the Christian quarter people were woken not by the peal of church bells but by the heavy silence that weighed upon the air. Nicias had spent the night in the Greek cemetery, on a slab the Turks had smashed. Surrounded by open graves and decomposing bodies that had been tipped from their caskets and piled up like so much human garbage, he had scarcely slept. In one tomb somebody had tried to hide a sewing machine, in another, a magic lantern; a third concealed an antique zither, and an amphora from the sixth century BC bearing an image of Heracles in his lionskin, aiming his bow at the monster Geryon.

Falling asleep with the *Odyssey* in his hand, Nicias saw the souls of the dead emerge from Erebus. They filed by as though in a procession: the young Greek men, the elders with beards long and short, the stabbed soldiers, the combatants with their throats cut like infidel dogs. Emerging from the darkness they began to drift to and fro, from the Lake of Oblivion to the Lake of Memory and back again. Disconsolate women roamed the abode of Hades the Invisible, clamoring for the justice that had not been delivered by mighty Hades or by Persephone, the goddess of terrible beauty. Faced with this procession of the dead, Nicias drew his sword in his dream and stood *en garde*, braced for the imminent Turkish assault. But then the soul of Tiresias appeared. The prophet of Thebes, raising his scepter, addressed him: "Why are you here, unhappy wretch? Why forsake the realms of light to gaze upon the dead?" Nicias lowered his sword and slid it back into the scabbard. He waited, but the hermaphrodite soothsayer said no more, his lips sewn together with invisible thread.

His slumber had been disturbed three times: first by the mournful souls of Greek soldiers trudging through fields of asphodels, while *chettes* flapped and squeaked around them like bats; then by the yells of the Turks pursuing their victims to the very edge of Tartarus, until checked by Hades in the helmet that rendered him invisible, his body floating through dark space; and the third time by the noise of gunshots coming from the Armenian quarter, where the massacre of Christians was continuing. Suddenly he shuddered to hear Cassandra's wail. In his dream Priam's daughter was a young Greek girl in torn clothes, with a punctured body and bleeding breasts. She was babbling crazily to herself, having been raped by the Turks in the night. Her fragile frame was broken, its lovely elements dislocated, the bones in splinters, the organs crushed. Nicias longed to place a mask over her face, to paint its eyelids and moisten its tears, to safeguard her, and to lavish kisses upon her profaned belly. He embraced her with respect, existentially and profusely. In gratitude she raised her fractured hand, straightened her shattered hip, and offered him her dancer's waist as a love token.

Among the cypresses and pine trees of the cemetery, an old lady who reminded him of Penelope, his mother, told Nicias more about the *chettes*' attack on the Armenian quarter. They had poured down the streets and alleyways, smashing doors and windows. Before entering a house, they would yell, "Out with you, stop hiding like mice! What are you scared of? If you don't come out we'll go in and kill you all!"

A pair of adolescent Armenian girls who had been cowering in the attic of their home, waiting for the bandits to be through plundering, were found, taken outside, and dragged to a nearby store to be abused. Nicias caught a passing glimpse of their Caucasian beauty, pale complexions, delicate noses, abundant down, and terrified eyes. For all their screams, nobody came to the rescue. They were taken through the streets, yet nobody saw. When they returned, their breasts had been cut off.

Late that evening, in the Greek quarter, Nicias encountered

Turkish civilians acting as spies for the cavalry. The blades of their scimitars seemed to widen as they curved away from the hilt and nearer to their victims' eyes.

"*Korkma! Korkma! Bir şey olmayacak!* Don't be afraid; nothing will happen to you!" shouted the soldiers to those indoors. On some of the facades, a relief carved in stone depicted the Armenian symbol of eternity.

Boulevard Resadiye was a street-long gibbet, an open-air morgue, an abattoir, strewn with slashed, hacked, violated humanity. Nicias placed his hand against doors, attentive to the pulsation of fallen bodies that feigned rigidity.

"*Korkma! Korkma!*" shouted the Turkish horsemen.

Nicias threw himself to the ground and played dead. A soldier was leaning out of the saddle, pricking at the wounded with a bayonet that pierced his back. The sharp point tore open his flesh. It was painful to breathe. Face down in the dirt he lay stock-still, in dread of being killed. Then he felt blood trickling down his ribs and surreptitiously touched the gash, which he judged was shallow.

While waiting for the soldier to ride away, he lay motionless, thinking back to the night when he himself bayoneted a *chette* against a wall and felt avenged for numberless offenses. How did he ever survive the deed, with hundreds of rabid *chettes* out to get him? He still couldn't comprehend it. Now the *chettes* were on the prowl. Clutching daggers shaped like crescent moons, hair clogged with sweat and blood, they seemed devoid of pity. And when they galloped on white steeds towards the pier, they resembled the horsemen of the Apocalypse.

He hid from them. Camouflaged against a wall, he lifted his

face to the stars. Before the astounding infinity of night, he felt equal to a god or a dog, because divinities and beasts dwell in the eternity of the moment, and he dwelt in the eternity of fear.

A whinny let him know that the *chette* chief and his gang were sacking homes nearby. Shouts could be heard from the Grand Boulevard.

"Have you been to the harbor?" Nicias asked an injured man.

"There are no boats to Chios," the stranger replied in an Armenian accent.

"I am seeking a different island."

"Are you a Greek?"

"I am."

"You won't be able to leave Smyrna. The Turks are hunting Christians down, and the boats that could take you away may never come."

"This is my country."

"If this is your country, you will only leave it in death."

"I will get out alive."

"Keep away from the Armenian quarter, and don't go near the Greek one either." The man hauled himself into his barber's shop.

When the interior became visible, Nicias saw a naked woman in the barber's chair. Her breasts had been sliced off, and one red strap sandal (the other foot was bare) balanced on the footrest. Her throat had been cut with a shaving razor.

"My name is Aram." The Armenian closed the door and the woman disappeared from view.

"Goodbye." Nicias got to his feet and began walking towards the harbor.

A military cortege was approaching. Mustafa Kemal rode in front in an open car, advancing between two long lines of trotting cavalry soldiers, with swords drawn and rifles propped against their shoulders. He was strangely silent in spite of the clatter of hooves. Strangely isolated, notwithstanding his retinue of worshippers. He was guarded by cavalry commanders, infantry, artillery, and assault troops as he went towards the Konak.

"*Antichristus cruentus,*" an Armenian cried at him, and the man with the icy stare blasted him with a glance before his soldiers did the rest.

Shortly afterward an officer and two soldiers with bayonets fitted to their barrels would drive to the Greek Cathedral to conduct Archbishop Chrysostomos to the Konak.

The metropolitan in his black robes would be roughly hustled out of his office and taken before General Nureddin Pasha, Kemal's recently appointed First Army commander. After a brief exchange, Chrysostomos would be accused of pro-Hellenism and delivered into the hands of the populace.

From the house of a blind man, Nicias followed the lynching scene.

"What is happening at that hairdresser's?" the blind man asked.

"The mob is putting a white apron on the archbishop. Seating him in a chair. Beating him with fists and clubs. The metropolitan is kicking. His eyes are being gouged out, his nose cut off, his ears and hands also; his beard is being yanked out by the roots. Now his body is being dragged to the Turkish quarter, to be thrown to the dogs by the crowd."

"And the church icons?"

"Flung into the street. The icons of Christ Pantocrator and Maria Theotokos have been desecrated, for whoever hates mankind also hates his gods."

"Do I hear the sound of a motorcar?" the blind man asked.

"That is the French soldiers who wanted to intervene on behalf of Chrysostomos, but their commander prevented them at gunpoint. They were forced to remain neutral."

"I recognize those *chettes* by the way they walk. What are they planning?"

"They have captured Jurukdoglou, the editor of *La Réforme*. He was found behind his car, head smashed on the cobbles. They also took the newspapers that were on the back seat: *L'Impérial, Journal de Smyrne, Amaltheia, Kosmos, The Orient News, Kopanos,* and *La Réforme*. They stuffed a message into his mouth: 'Eat them.'"

LA PHRYGIE

Nicias had been a regular at this taverna since the night of the Greek landing, and it was here that he used to meet Eurydice. Sometimes she came with Calliope, who lived in a nearby small town. Calliope was hoping to move to Smyrna with her daughter Artemis, now that the child's father had gone to try his luck in America. Eurydice often told Nicias her recurrent dream about Apollonius of Tyana, a dream set in Cappadocia. The sage and miracle worker—who, Philostratus tells us, rose from the dead to heal the sick, traveled to distant lands as far as India, and ascended bodily to heaven—was to save her from the hell we all carry within.

At the taverna door Nicias remembered Eurydice saying to him: "A Greek in Turkey bears death on his eyelashes. Be as crafty as Odysseus."

"Where did love go?" Nicias wondered to his reflection in the mirror.

"Turkish women have no lips, only teeth; they open their mouths to bite, not kiss. They don't know how to smile," the taverna keeper told him. "Never forget it: Smyrnean women have skulls in place of breasts."

An English pastor was describing the latest outrage to the Greek landlord: "When the Turkish soldiers burst into his house in Bournabat, they assured the octogenarian Dr. Murphy that he had nothing to fear: they weren't going to hurt anybody; they only wanted to rape the women, demolish the furniture, and do a little looting. His two daughters hid upstairs and were safe; but the young maidservant took the fancy of those lecherous blackguards and was dragged away, though she clung desperately to the doctor's knees, imploring him to protect her. When Murphy tried to stop them, the soldiers beat him about the head, shot him in the shoulders, stabbed him, and wounded him with their muskets. Leaving him for dead, they smashed up the piano. They hated music, they said, and went off with a chest full of British Treasury banknotes, American dollars, and Austrian gold crowns. The young servant was raped and killed."

"Aren't you the Reverend Charles Dobson, the Anglican chaplain at Smyrna?" asked Nicias.

"How did you know?"

"You are a familiar face around town."

"Shall I tell you something? The metropolitan gave me an urgent message for the Archbishop of Canterbury. It enjoined him in Christ's name to exert his influence on the British Cabinet to guarantee the safety of the population, should Kemal enter the city. I took it to the British authorities, and the naval chief of staff. Admiral Sir Osmond de Beauvoir Brock said he would protect 'all sections of the community' and told me I could give the message to the press. I deeply regret having left that message sitting on my desk. I don't know why I'm telling you this—perhaps because I now wish I had sent it . . . but I was afraid. Do you hear that hullabaloo? A short while ago, in that street, a woman fell to her knees before me begging protection, until a Turkish squadron came along with rifles and sabers and went past me, so as not to strike the woman. . . . But further along I heard shooting: Turkish civilians were beginning to attack the Greek refugees. Be careful how you go; carnage and rape are spreading everywhere; even the nationals of the Great Powers are at risk. The best way to kill a Turk is with a blade, so as to save on bullets."

Reverend Dobson walked off down the street.

Monday, September 11. Nureddin Pasha ordered the extermination of the Armenians, and their quarter was surrounded. Squads of Turkish soldiers combed the area, hunting down the men and abducting the women. The dead and dying were left where they fell, and when an old man begged for his life on his knees, they chopped off his hands. The *chettes* plundered and torched the Bournabat mansions of Levantine merchants; several residents of the suburb witnessed the slaughter of twenty-six young maidservants who had first been raped.

In the Greek quarter, Turkish soldiers with Mongolian faces, portraits of Mustafa Kemal pinned to their fezzes, ravaged private houses. They defiled graves and kicked over crosses in the cemetery. They lined up Greek prisoners of war on the pier and forced them to shout: "Long life to Mustafa Kemal!"

The captives bellowed the words like wounded bulls. Nicias said to himself: "Don't utter that name, don't summon up demons, call him the Unnamable."

Now that the streets leading to the Armenian quarter had been closed off, men and women sought refuge in St. Stepanos Cathedral. Its vaulted ceiling floated as if suspended in the air, and its gilded icons glittered as if in celebration. Down the lamp-lit central nave moved the faithful, carrying pectoral crosses, chalices, and reliquaries, and chanting liturgical hymns, while women lit candles beneath the icon of Our Lady, praying for the safe return of sons herded away by the Turks on a "works detail"—in full knowledge that they would never come back.

Buoyed by percussion instruments, cymbals, and bells, the voice of a cobbler's son rebounded from wall to wall; he called himself Komitas, after the Armenian composer and priest who had been deported in 1915. All of a sudden Turkish soldiers burst into the church with guns, sabers, and grenades to use against the "infidel dogs" sheltering inside. They slashed the priest's throat as he knelt before the altar, and scythed the choir with bayonets as they scattered through the naves.

The killing continued in the atrium and in among the trees, pilasters, walls, and railings. It spilled into the street, where the *chettes* lay in wait for the fleeing and the injured, ready to steal clothes, money, and valuables. The scene evoked a fresco of the massacre of the innocents, with human devils spearing children wrapped in flames. But the thugs were not slaked until they had silenced the voice of the cantor Komitas, as though with it they sought to extinguish the soul of the *tagher*, the liturgical chants of the medieval Armenian Church.

Pallid girls huddling in the apse were violated in front of their fathers and husbands, who watched with brimming eyes as the *chettes* stripped them naked, tore out their hair, and disfigured their faces under the impassive gaze of the commander who had ordered the massacre. But what also moved Nicias was to see the old pine tree on fire in front of the church facade. Flames crackled through the gnarled trunk from root to tip as though the tree were speaking, while the air of nearby groves grew pungent with the heavy scent of resin. When the great pine had burned to the ground, and the stones glowed candescent as burning amber, Nicias grieved for the loss of the congregation and for the tree.

By the fence he found two Armenian girls on the ground, left lying by the Turks with gashed stomachs and breasts. He could do no more than place his handkerchief over the face of one whose eyes were open.

"Pape Satàn, pape Satàn aleppe!" In the sacristy Nureddin Pasha seemed to be invoking a biblical demon as he repeated

the words that Dante put in Plutus's mouth. His thick black brows jutted over his glacial gaze; his beard was dripping blood. The sound of his striding boots was like the creak of a vampire's casket lid as it lifts. The church cat hid when it saw him approach.

Nicias wondered: "What is the impaler doing in this sacred space?" But then he saw two soldiers pulling a young Armenian woman down the corridor into an adjacent room, where they flung her onto the bed with her skirts over her face. She had been injured trying to resist. On the wall hung the hide of a feline, with empty eye sockets and mutilated ears.

"Ephesus, Smyrna, Pergamum, Thyatira, Sardis, Philadelphia, Laodicea." Nicias recited the names of the seven churches of Asia. "I am Alpha and Omega, the beginning and the ending, saith the Lord, which is, and which was, and which is to come, the Almighty."

"Al-Dajjal." The door to the room where Nureddin Pasha had joined the girl was closed by a Turkish soldier with shrunken canines, like a syphilitic. His cruel eye (he had only one) boded death, and Nicias cravenly bowed his head.

In the fig market Nicias came across a young girl with a shattered gaze, slumped against a small ladder, her body hatched with wounds. The nascent, bruised nipples resembled the sultana grapes his father used to grow in Tire.

"What happened to her?" Nicias asked a man who was sitting in the roadway. His age was written on the vein-roped hands, and he had as many sunspots as years. Although plainly Armenian, he was wearing Turkish military medals.

"She was raped all night long by Turkish troops."

"How do you know?"

"I used to be her doctor. I've known her since she was small."

"What is your name?"

"Dr. Hatcherian."

"They killed her with appalling brutality."

"Only a diabolical mind could ever think to destroy such a lovely child. Her eyes are full of horror, as if the last thing she saw was the devil."

"What a courageous feat . . . a dead child."

"Kemal pays his bandit followers in kind."

"If the girls put up a fight, they die. If they don't, the outcome is the same."

"But there's nothing to worry about: the other day a Danish man whose wife and daughter were raped actually thanked the Turks for their consideration in penetrating the daughter from the rear, respecting her virginity."

"Vultures, they tore this child apart. Whoever hates woman also hates her genesis."

"See those horses over there with broken legs." The doctor pointed at the dead beasts, their heads impaled on stakes in the grass, as if on show, their huge eyes bulging from their sockets.

"They died in terror, as did the riders lying beside them."

"I feel for wounded animals; they can't understand what's happening."

"Don't look for tears in a dead man's eye, as they say in Asia Minor."

"Such is our fate on earth, to spit out our souls in blood, to drag ourselves like worms through the air," wailed the Armenian.

"Keep your voice down. Farewell."

"Farewell."

In the Greek quarter, soldiers were firing on Christian civilians. It was hard to tell the aggressors from the victims when all alike were shapeless forms in darkness, just as the walls that had crumbled under the shells could be mistaken for doors. Among the shadows the injured and the dead were gathered up by unknown hands. Not to rush them to a hospital but to make them disappear, to clear away all traces of their end.

The *chettes* stalked the narrow streets with shotguns and knives in each hand. They hunted women and children like so many chickens or rabbits. Drunk on death, they shot indiscriminately at bleeding bodies and through windows, mowing down pedestrians, chasing away snoopers, cutting throats at random. The war had spawned a new species of predator, one who murdered at whim. With his heart in his boots Nicias appreciated the aesthetic of cracked foundations, riddled walls, doors hanging off their hinges, and steps leading nowhere. The red hue of minarets blurred into that of poppy-colored clouds. The city's destruction was like an engraving by Piranesi, etched onto a decomposing sky. The garden of an ancient house suggested a dropped flower vase, yellow and purple and scarlet tulips crushed beneath the rubble.

"The tulips of Anatolia are hermaphrodites," he thought. "With their gynoecia and androecia, their free-waving tepals with tufts of white hairs at the apex, their turbans like phallic robes hollow inside, like female vulvas, those are our flowers, our Tiresiases." There were ragged, damaged shrubs at the end of the street, and the foliage and grass had been scorched with petroleum.

Behind the storefronts, smashed in by rifle-butts, the shadow of broken panes fell on soiled window display cloths. But there was nothing there: everything of value had been snatched. The bodies of the owners lay within, curled up on beds of cinders. On the counter sat a hand, in the corner a thigh; a hank of hair spilled from a drawer, as pale as if it had aged overnight. Ashes clogged the folds of men and women's buttocks, elbows, and knees, where the fluids of death gleamed gray. Outside, the ashes floated through the air or blew in from far away, wrapped in Black Sea breezes.

Groups of Turkish soldiers were seen bringing kerosene, gunpowder, bombs, and barrels of fuel from the Petroleum Company of Smyrna. People feared their plan was to set the city on fire.

A CHILDREN'S PARADISE

"Successor to Anastasio Zacuto. Proprietor," read the sign in the window of the oldest toyshop in Smyrna. It went on:

Permanent exhibition of toys and creatures with human
visage such as can only be met in dreams. See for yourself the
astounding progress of engineering, marvel at the blazing
building which firemen try in vain to extinguish, the fire

engine carrying petroleum drums equipped with ladders and flame-throwing hoses. All amazingly true to life.

Visit the Magicians' Bazaar. Thrill to the pictures projected into empty space by magic lanterns and by our vast assortment of future weapons of circular repercussion, which after revolving around the shooter turn against his own body.

Nicias stood transfixed before the window of this curiosity shop. Here were such wondrous items as a mermaid with female breasts and a dolphin's tail, and a box of De Gruyters cocoa decorated with a smiling little girl sitting on a pack of chocolates. He gazed just as intently at the cardboard Pegasus with golden wings, and the harpy with a woman's face and bird's body, who, if wound up by a tiny key, would begin to gyrate like a belly dancer; he gazed at the merry centaur with his dark bow and silvery arrows that sparkled in the air and disappeared. All these playthings were bathed in the yellowish glow of an incandescent lamp, the light of childhood, which slowly kindled an aching nostalgia in him. He had inadvertently found himself in the midst of the mythology that had brightened many a dreary afternoon for him as a boy, within what was also a store selling modern products like the candies the older generation of Greeks called *amygdalae pecuniae*, money almonds. And, for the first time in his life, these childish toys and everyday treats—in present circumstances, almost the products of memory—seemed to him as vulnerable as his own existence, both of them steeped in an undefinable melancholy.

The neighborhood was a maze of truncated alleyways and cul-de-sacs, of crooked lines, and doors and windows swinging loose, and sudden pits like mental as well as visual traps. This twisted geometry of history caused him great anguish, not only because of the abundance of riddled walls and violently breached thresholds; it was the topography of a man-made hell.

And faced with this derelict landscape, his body seemed to shudder inside, although his legs and hands were still.

"Ha-ha-ha," cackled an emaciated *chette*. The saber in his skeletal fingers jabbed at the sky as if trying to slice the air. With bleary eyes, broken teeth, a pointed goatee, and a lantern wedged on his head like a crown, he was sauntering out of a male brothel, delighted at having gutted a dainty Greek youth.

"Bang bang, rat-a-tat-a-tat," yelled a trio of Turkish teenagers, playing at killing Greek children with wooden guns.

"Boom-boom-boom!" Three Turkish lads in black imitated the shots.

"Bang bang, rat-a-tat-a-tat," giggled the skeleton.

"Ra-ta-tat-a-tat," echoed the terrified Greek children under duress, flat on the ground with their arms over their heads.

"Ha ha ha!" went the skeleton, and slipped into a ruined hotel. He mounted the stairs like a shadow. Like a reptile he crept along the passage. He was downstairs in one hop and swaggered outside. He told the driver of a black car to take him to the Konak.

"That's the police chief. He says he's going to the Konak but he's really off to the buggery club," said one youth to another. Both of them had put a *haik* over their bodies, playing at being girls.

Nicias followed him down a street buzzing with tavernas and popular cafés. The bodies of the dissolute young men that hung around there smacked of sea salt.

The police chief entered a male brothel deep in a back alley. Its dingy, squalid rooms were hidden away above a sordid bar full of tipsy sailors, whooping, dancing, and playing cards.

A man dressed in black glanced down through a dimly lit window. His eyes were rimmed with kohl, his lips rouged, and his nipples were orange-red as if spiced with saffron. Was it him? Or was it an artillery chief with a notorious taste for the flesh of dead ephebes and for hacking live ones to pieces? His head and neck were reminiscent of the vulture *Sarcogyps calvus*, especially when he craned forward, as now, drunk on voluptuousness, to sink his beak into an adolescent navel.

The drape fell back. The figure moved to another room, perhaps the seraglio where the Turkish officers kept Greek youths and Armenian girls for their personal use.

CHEZ FRINÉ

This was the name of the dive across the street.

A vitrine contained a painting of Phryne, the Thespian hetaira who was tried by the Areopagus. Naked and slender, her face that of a toad, she knelt at the feet of a hermaphrodite Tiresias with lascivious eyes.

A poster on the vestibule wall advertised a belly-dancing performance by Eurydice Andrakis. Livid spotlights accented her thick lips, erect nipples, and rosy belly button as the woman struck an obscene pose that synchronized the lilt of pelvis, hips, and torso with the strains of some absent music. Legs splayed, feet bare, she was tracing figures of eight with a salacious rictus on her face.

"They look the same but they're different; there are small but great differences between the two," Nicias said to himself. "The Eurydice Andrakis I knew in Smyrna and the belly dancer on the poster have nothing whatsoever in common. The dancer has sagging breasts, black eyes and hair, mauve stomach and thighs; the Eurydice I remember has high-riding breasts, chestnut eyes and hair, and her thighs and belly are like milk. But the all-important difference is that the woman on the poster transmits vulgarity, vulgarity, vulgarity from every feature; whereas the girl I remember, even when she's naked, expresses innocence."

There was a reproduction of Caravaggio's *Medusa* on the wall. However fearsome this monster's glaring eyes, serpent locks, and bloody mouth and neck, for Nicias the extremity of terror was not the depiction of the beheaded Gorgon but rather the *chettes*, those two-legged snakes prowling the streets of Smyrna with eyes so evil that they turned little girls into stones.

The first things he saw in the bar's dens and toilets were stolen carpets and broken mirrors. And the grubby residues of sex for money. It was thoroughly depressing. Then he noticed a girl standing in a low black doorway, wearing a slip and green sandals that matched her green hair.

"I'm Eurydice; tell me what you want," said the embodiment of the woman in the poster. "Aren't you the fastest blind dancer in Smyrna?"

"I can dance, and dance well, but in Smyrna I dance with death."

"I am your friend."

"You are not my friend."

"Take a look through that window at the blazing city; see the thousands of men and women setting out for gloomy Anatolia."

"I don't want to see it."

"Grrrrrr," and she leaped at him, brandishing pointed nails on outstretched hands. She opened her mouth as if hungry to bite his lips.

Nicias walked away down a narrow corridor.

AU JARDIN

"To the Garden," said the sign on the wall. But there was no garden. There was a staircase, an unfurnished room, and a vacant lot dotted with open graves. Skeletons in Turkish dress lay with stakes driven through their chests and mouths.

"Those are the *vrykolakas*, the vampires of Lesbos. The legend says that since the fall of Constantinople they emerge periodically from hell to drink the blood of Greek children; but don't be scared, they're just Sultan Mehmet's bastard sons," the woman gabbled.

"Do I hear voices in the bar? Are there people coming in?"

"Only the agents of the boss of the police department. They're looking for Greeks to kill, but don't you worry; you're not a Greek; you'll only have to answer a few questions and they'll let you go."

The voices and footsteps grew louder. In his haste to get away Nicias pushed the wrong door, to an annex rather than the street.

"You're caught," said the woman at his heels.

But he did not stop. He went through crumbling walls and across dance floors under deathly lights. Among the chairs he found an Armenian couple. Impaled, embracing, their hair spread over the broken glasses and plates.

By the bar, a man sagged with a bayonet through his chest. He was about fifty, although he looked eighty. Nicias remembered the summer he had arrived from Alexandria. A chatterbox in life, now his teeth were smashed in. He was the owner of Chez Friné. A dog-eared travel guide was in his hand: "The Mediterranean. Seaports and sea routes, including Smyrna. With 38 maps and 49 plans. Baedeker, Leipzig, 1911." On one of the plans somebody had replaced the word Smyrna with the word Izmir. A date was scrawled in red ink: "September 13, 1922."

The same unknown hand had blotted the Cavafy poem on the wall with blood:

Ionic

That we've broken their statues,
that we've driven them out of their temples,
doesn't mean at all that the gods are dead.
O land of Ionia, they're still in love with you,
their souls still keep your memory.
When an August dawn wakes over you,
your atmosphere is potent with their life,

and sometimes a young ethereal figure,

indistinct, in rapid flight,

wings across your hills.[3]

"Take that corridor and don't look back. Turkish agents have surrounded the Greek quarter; they have come in army trucks; you're a marked man." Calliope appeared by his side. "There's a secret door in the kitchen. Don't make a sound, and throw that pistol away; it's empty."

"Can you tell me where Eurydice is?"

"I'll let her know."

"Stop or I'll shoot!" Nicias heard a Turk shouting outside. The sound of running feet.

"You go ahead. I'll wait for Eurydice," said Calliope as she disappeared.

Birds were fluttering in the kitchen, knocking against the windows. Inside a cage with twisted bars other, charred, birds lay, the kind the residents of Smyrna were fond of eating in the hunting season. Nicias fell ravenously on the chicken wings and feet he found in a skillet. He chewed stale bread from one of the Greek bakeries closed by order of the Turks. Glancing outside he saw injured people in the rubble, dead bodies on the ground. He could jump out of that window if danger threatened. The Turkish agents' truck disappeared around the corner. He watched tensely for its return.

Just then Eurydice stepped from a secret room. Her hair was

---

[3] Konstantinos Kavafis, *C. P. Cavafy: Collected Poems*, trans. Edmund Keeley and Philip Sherrard, ed. George Savidis (Princeton: Princeton University Press, 1975), 33.

loose and her eyes were shining, her body half naked. She took his arm.

"My soul desires you more ardently than ever . . . not even when together we plowed the watery main . . . did I burn as I do now to love you and make you mine," he said to her in Homeric words. And drew her toward the bed. And she followed her lover.

Their clothing discarded, each reveled in the other, the memory of past encounters blending into the fresh contact of caresses and curves, kisses and compulsions. Urgency merged with serenity.

"These instants that seem hours yield joy in the midst of hell, a wave of tenderness among explosions, a brief interruption of the catastrophe. But where are you, Eurydice? Is it truly you who is loving me? Are you truly her?" As Nicias thought these things he wondered how much time the fates would grant them, how long they would be able to keep death at bay behind the door, for well he knew that the *chettes* were searching the Greek quarter to find and kill him.

Unable to get his fill of her, Nicias regarded the filigree of veins beneath the translucent skin, the soft breasts like a pair of trembling doves, the hair that rippled under his caress as in an old poem. Until at last he fell asleep; and woke, to find she was not there, gone from his side with mysterious stealth.

Nicias went to the window. Hundreds of men were trudging down the interminable street, their eyes fixed on nothingness. He imagined himself amongst them. A black moon appeared on the wall of the facing house. The starlings high above took the form of phantoms. He walked with the men until wrenching his body with his eyes out of the multitude of deportees.

Parties of *chettes* marched behind the procession, hollering tuneless patriotic songs. An explosion. A string of explosions scattered them over the sidewalks. A rattle of machine guns was heard. It was not clear who was killing whom. Supernatural legions were massed in Smyrna to wage a battle against mankind, Nicias thought.

"We meet again, Kyriakos Melisurgos." Out in the street, the Turkish officer was pointing a gun at him.

"My name is Demetrios Philhellenos," he replied.

"Ah, what a surprise; you've changed your name!"

"What's the matter?" Nicias demanded of a yellow-eyed *chette* who was looking him up and down, knife in fist, as if deciding how best to carve.

"Every face conceals a secret. I want to see yours."

"Your secret is why you kill."

"That secret is why I want to cut your eyes out." The drunken *chette* could barely open his mouth to speak.

"Ah." The officer's attention was distracted by a Turkish civilian who tossed a flaming carpet out of a window before emerging from the house, dragging an Armenian adolescent behind him. The assailant yanked her hands out of the folds of the thick cloths her mother had wrapped her in, like a doll. As he started to strip her he noticed her pockets were sewn fast, concealing money, and he would need a knife to get at it.

At this point Nicias bolted.

* * *

He wandered through the streets looking at movie theater facades and was drawn especially to those picture houses where he had once seen a film: the Smyrna (or American) Theater, the Pathé, the Alhambra with its arched portico, the Parision, the Café de Paris, the Cine Pallas, the Melis. In their auditoriums Nicias had traveled to distant cities, carried away by idylls and dramas and far-fetched adventure stories; he had laughed along with Charlie Chaplin and taken *A Trip to the Moon* with Méliès. Above all he had gone away, away from Turkey. He came to know Lucifer and the nine circles of Dante's Hell in *L'Inferno*, *Fantômas* kept him in suspense in France, he lived through *The Last Days of Pompeii*, he learned about the American Civil War watching *The Birth of a Nation*. *The Golem* and *The Student of Prague* had whisked him into magical cities inhabited by Jewish cabalists and supernatural beings.

Nicias was intrigued by the movie advertised outside the Cine Pallas: *Nosferatu: A Symphony of Horror*. This and other billed features aroused his interest, but he was not sure whether he could bear them in his current frame of mind. Besides, no doubt the screenings had been cancelled. The spectators would be too fearful of packs of *chettes* bursting into the theaters, like Ottoman wolves from gray and craggy Anatolia.

A fresh sea breeze relieved the afternoon heat. The starlings, bunched under the sky like black racemes, suddenly streaked for the mountains of the bay.

Outside the Smyrna Theater a sandwich man paced back and forth, two boards hanging from straps over his shoulders. The front placard read as follows:

SMYRNA
Turkish History Play in Four Parts
Designed and Staged by General Nureddin Pasha

The Great Butcher
At the orders of Mustafa Kemal
Guests of Honor: Admiral Mark Bristol
and
The Captains of the Allied Warships

The back read:

A Blood-Curdling Spectacle
A Hair-Raising Experience
Not suitable for Children

Entrance Free
Exit Forbidden
Not to be Missed

Smyrna, City of Tolerance. September 9 to 14, 1922

The performance was due to begin at 7 p.m. But the play was already taking place in the city. A detachment of sailors was guarding some three hundred native and naturalized American citizens waiting to be evacuated on the destroyers. Inside the theater, all seemed quiet: no music, voices, or footsteps could be heard, nor could any lights be detected. Turkish forces patrolled the adjoining streets, to stop any Greeks or Armenians from gaining access to the theater.

Nicias walked past the human billboard towards the entrance. On finding the doors bolted and a Turkish soldier observing him through a peephole, he retreated, affecting to study the slow movement of the hands of a clock on the wall. There he might have lingered, had not a gang of *chettes* congregated on the corner with bags of stolen jewelry from the stores of the Armenian A. Balladur and the Greeks Ioannis Righo and Konstantinos Georgiadis. He recognized the marauders by their coarse attire and manners, their curling mustaches and rustic fezzes, their insolent way of carrying a gun. Three of them had lined up some human heads on a table. He stared at them and they stared back, in light of which he decided to make himself scarce.

Nicias glanced up from the street at the cockerel, which was the emblem of the Pathé Cinema, and stepped inside via a hole in the wall. He passed the deserted box office and crossed the lobby over threadbare carpets to reach the wrecked auditorium itself. There, like a character escaped from a movie, he saw a Greek officer advance down a flaking corridor towards him, holding a stolen gun, hungry and weary, eyes darting mistrustfully about.

Nicias watched the stranger step down to the auditorium—cautiously, because the steps were littered with debris, and fearfully, so as not to make noise. He halted beside a row of seats and began to declaim in a dramatic voice the opening lines of *The Bacchantes*:

I am come to this land of Thebes, Dionysus the son of Zeus, of whom on a day Semele, the daughter of Cadmus, was delivered by a flash of lightning. . . . O'er Persia's sun-baked plains . . . have I advanced.[4]

"I don't know what to say," Nicias put in.

"We are the victims of a plot hatched by gods in whom we no longer believe, because they abandoned us in our hour of greatest need."

"I don't understand."

"Would you understand if I told you we were two characters staring into each other's eyes, gripped by a mutual hallucination? Don't you remember me? We fought together in Thrace and Trebizond."

"So?"

"Do you remember Lumière's film *Arrival of a Train at La Ciotat*? There's a station platform with people walking around and a train seems to come flying out of the frame, head-on, at the camera. The train of the film is like history coming off the rails and straight into us."

"There's nothing on this screen; the projector's out of order."

"The only thing that still works is the hatchet the Turks used to destroy that black piano."

"I see an Armenian couple in the back row, and a child sitting on the floor. Am I right?"

---

[4]Euripedes, *The Bacchantes* (Cambridge, MA: The Internet Classics Archive by Daniel C. Stevenson, Web Atomics, 2000), http://classics.mit.edu/Euripides/bacchan.html.

"Why should you doubt your own eyes?"

"Lately I've been uncertain about anything I see, hear, or say."

"You can't doubt the reality of that black-eyed woman who is watching us."

"Stay, don't be afraid," Nicias said to the woman as she made to run away.

"The last boat to Samos will be leaving soon; you can come with me," the officer said to the Armenians.

"All the ships have gone," the woman murmured.

"Ship or no ship, I'm off to Samos." The officer lurched crazily towards the exit, rifle at the ready. "My destiny will not hail from Olympus or from Hades, but from twilight Anatolia with her wolf face and goat smell. The man who will pierce me through the heart is nobody I know; I neither love nor hate him. My people are the poor of Asia Minor. Once he has slain me he will be neither worse nor better, just a poor devil with blood-stained hands who will melt back into the host of nameless assassins from whence he came."

"Drop the gun; they'll kill you," Nicias called after him. Too late: a Turkish sniper aimed at his chest, and the officer fell down on the cobblestones.

Standing beside the body, Nicias saw that the iconic Pathé cockerel above the awning had had its head blown off.

At that moment Calliope's daughter Artemis swiftly pressed a piece of paper into his hand before vanishing into a dried fruits and nuts store. The message from Calliope read: "Eurydice is waiting in Bayrakli. At the spot where the ancient kore looks without seeing."

As though the film's action were continuing offscreen—a silent movie in which the extras were ordinary townspeople going about their business—he walked down Frank Street.

Like a camera his eye recorded successive situations-moments-faces in the here and now, whether the distant tremor of the bay or a tree stripped of leaves in a bombed-out street, the cratered walls of an Armenian home, the bare feet of a brace of Greek prisoners being conducted to the Konak for execution, a Greek family in a cart pulled by a blinkered horse, or a father and daughter laid out side by side in a burial box. He registered with equal clarity a *chette* grasping a child by the wrist the better to stab her, and an old lady rocking someone else's baby in her arms, a knot of troops firing on women and children, and four Turks mounted on white Cappadocian steeds. He saw a mural depicting Abdülhamid—the Red Sultan, alias the Butcher alias the Murderer alias the Scourge of Children alias the Vrykolakas Vampire—and seven goats' heads on a platter with skinned teeth and staring eyes, the trembling of his own hands caused by inner repugnance at the death of the goats, a lighter crammed with refugees, and a human head with a hole between the eyes, placed on a shelf by a Turk. His camera-vision recorded all these scenes while time seemed alternately to accelerate and to slow down, not in the streets but within himself, not in his feet but in his eyes. Thus, Nicias filmed on in his mind, until he came upon a dead man who resembled him; perhaps it was his double, or perhaps the Greek officer in the torn uniform.

Up on the rocks Nicias then spied a group of *chettes* in the shape of vultures and winged hyenas, picking over the bones, skin, and sinews of the recently deceased. Quarrelsome, hairy, and bald, they sank their clawless talons into the entrails of the Armenian woman from the cinema. At last, as if the woman were falling down the black cliff-face of history, he came back to himself in the middle of the road.

Tuesday, September 12. The ships were there. The captains of yesterday and tomorrow focused their binoculars on the refugees, and snapped pictures to keep as souvenirs of the "moments" of exodus and calamity. The officers had orders from Admiral Bristol, the US high commissioner in Constantinople, not to intervene, to stand passively by throughout the massacres of Greeks and Armenians in Smyrna and elsewhere in Asia Minor.

The city was built at the head of the gulf. Beyond the pincers formed like arms by the peninsula and the mainland, the coast of Lesbos was visible. In the port Nicias was riveted by the spectacle of those Allied vessels, knowing their masters cared more for their countries' commercial, military, and diplomatic interests than for saving lives. He had a clear view of the names, insignia, flags, and numbers. Here was the British flagship HMS *Iron Duke*, along with the *King George V*, *Cardiff*, and *Serapis*; the American destroyers *Winona*, *Litchfield*, *Lawrence*, and *Simpson*; the French vessels *Phrygie*, *Jean Bart*, and *Tonkinois*; the *Sardegna* and the *Bavarian*. Finally, there were other vessels whose names were so illegible it seemed they did not wish to be identified. Most appeared to be coming into harbor, as though to pick up refugees; but they did not move; the crews had been sternly briefed against lending succor.

"Take a good look at those Allied ships, indifferent witnesses to mass slaughter on Homeric soil. Remember their names when you arrive in other lands," murmured Alexis Seferiades over his shoulder.

"I see their outlines, names, and numbers," Nicias replied. "First I see the USS *Litchfield* with its cargo of Americans, ready to bear refugees away from the raging fire. I am looking at it from out at sea, against the backdrop of the city with its white billows of smoke and windows like crackling eyeballs."

"The number 336 stands out," Seferiades said, "beneath the small letters of the name. She was laid down on January 15, 1919, by the Mare Island Navy Yard, and launched on August 12 that same year. Sponsored by Mrs. Martha D. Litchfield, the mother of pharmacist's mate John Litchfield, she left San Diego in late 1921, and after the annual fleet maneuvers joined Division 39, bound for the Mediterranean. She reached Constantinople on June 28, 1922. Under the direct command of Admiral Bristol, she resembles a beast of black steel, blind to atrocity. Her sleek hull is impervious to the screams and gesticulations that arrive in gusts from the crowds lifting their arms to heaven while their city is devoured by the flames.

"I can make out the SS *Winona*, completed in New Jersey in 1919. She is a steam merchant with a tonnage of 6.197, which will leave for Piraeus on September 14 with 350 refugees on board. The *Simpson*, number 221, has a long dark hull and prominent guns. Now the wind is dispersing black smoke from her four funnels. She was laid down on October 9, 1919, by William Cramp and Sons of Philadelphia, and launched on April 28, 1920, by Miss Caroline Sterett Simpson, the daughter of Rear Admiral Simpson. Commissioned on November 3 of that year, she sailed to the Mediterranean in June 1922. Her crew is poised to evacuate US citizens and convey them to Greece.

"USS *Lawrence* is long and narrow as a lizard. Her guns are primed to fire, and her armored turrets and white funnels with dark rings make her look like a marine mirage made of ripples combed by the breeze. The number 250 is visible from the shore. The flag flutters over the prow. I can see officers standing on the bridge, their binoculars trained on me. The *Lawrence* is a bitter hulk of a gunboat, assigned to the Destroyer Force Atlantic Fleet, which left Newport for the Mediterranean on June 13 this year. She reached Constantinople on July 4 to join up with the naval forces.

"And there is the dreadnought HMS *Iron Duke*, christened in honor of Arthur Wellesley, first Duke of Wellington, whose nickname it was. We have a good view of her central battery, with ten naval gus mounted in five turrets. Her motto is 'Virtutis fortuna comes' (Fortune is the companion of valor). Her skipper enjoys listening to band music and comic operas against a background of mayhem and the smell of roasting flesh.

"The designs of USS *Edsall*, DD-219, are inscrutable. Launched on July 29, 1920, by William Cramp and Sons, the *Edsall* left Philadelphia for San Diego on December 6, 1920. In May 1922 she was dispatched to the Mediterranean, and arrived at Constantinople on June 28. When the Turks set Smyrna on fire, the *Edsall* will be one of the destroyers evacuating thousands of Greek refugees. On September 14 it is due to carry hundreds of refugees from the *Litchfield* to Salonika, and it will return to Smyrna on the sixteenth to command the naval forces. I should mention that it is not quite visible yet, but I already discern its keel and funnels and guns, with the bay for a backdrop."

"Stop right there," Nicias broke in. "The silhouettes of these ghost ships softly rocking in my vision make me dizzy."

"Now say, O Muses of Hades' Mansion, who captained the galleons?" Professor Seferiades was recalling Homer's catalogue of Achaean ships: "Fifty ships, and on board of each came one hundred and twenty young men of the Boeotians. . . . Born in the house of Actor, son of Azeus; Astyoche, the honored maiden, gave them life, conceived of mighty Ares, who lay with her in secret in her chamber. Thirty ships were ranged with these. . . . Forty black ships followed, and their leaders marshalled them to the left flank of the Boeotians. . . . King Agamemnon bestowed sixty black and well-appointed ships wherewith to cross the wine-dark sea, for of seafaring they knew little. . . . And Odysseus led the Cephallenians, great-souled warriors from Ithaca and Neritum. . . . And with him came eighty black ships. . . . And with they that held Tricca were ranged thirty hollow ships. . . . Forty black ships sail to their destiny. . . ."[5] "And rosy-fingered dawn spoke in her splendor, not in words."

"I can't understand, Professor, why in a time of such tribula-

---

[5] Homer, *La Iliada de Homero,* traslado de Alfonso Reyes (México: Fondo de Cultura Económica, 1951), 50–58. (Translated from this edition by Lorna Scott Fox.)

tion for the Greeks you start reciting the catalogue of Achaean ships bound for Troy," Nicias said irritably.

"It is so that you never forget the origins of the Greeks now being massacred by the Turks. How I wish that those Achaean fleets could appear before my eyes! I would go calmly to my death, secure in the knowledge that Homeric justice exists."

"The ship sailed out of harbor," Nicias said, as if hallucinating. "A blood-tinged breeze plucked at her rigging. A phantom crew bent to oar along her flanks and hoisted the sails so as to race more quickly into the waiting storm. The ship sliced the water and from old Aeolia on the coast of Asia Minor an eager wind began to blow. The stars glittered in the vault of the sea."

The day was bright, the scene appalling. The *chettes* were plundering the Christian neighborhoods, taking all the time in the world to select the most valuable booty from the smart shops on Frank Street. The Turkish security patrols looked the other way. Corpses lay uncovered in the sun, their backs and shoulders notched and gashed. Young maidservants who had been abused lay outside their front doors like war trophies. Stripped naked, with bloody abdomens, bruised thighs, and slashed breasts, they were like votive offerings to Turkish misogyny. The stench of decomposing flesh drifted over the cobbles.

"Look out," said an Armenian man to Nicias. An officer was skulking in a doorway.

"*Pasaport*," barked the Turk.

"I've lost it," Nicias said. With any luck he'd be able to vanish into the throng heading for the American Collegiate Institute, where thousands of refugees were already camped out in the grounds. If luck failed, he would be captured.

"*Kafir, kafir!* Infidel," shouted the officer as Nicias made his getaway.

On the quayside Nicias met a heaving crowd of refugees. Some had their arms full with infants and bundles; others pushed sick relatives in barrows. A man and a little girl were pulling a dead woman like a sack of potatoes. When a boat was spotted, the people hurled themselves at the waterfront railings to tear them down.

"There are no refugees here," said an assault troops commander, pointing up a deserted street. "Nothing but unclaimed luggage."

"May neither Sea nor Earth receive your body when you are dead." Nicias cursed him in the words of Euripides, which the officer did not understand.

"Keep moving!" yelled an infantry commander at a woman lying prostrate in a stretcher, with a baby in her arms.

"Please, let my husband through!" She didn't want to go forward, because her man had been detained, but the Turk pointed his rifle at her.

Hundreds of thousands of refugees had already gathered in the city, and demoralized Greek soldiers kept arriving. They camped in the streets, on the beaches, and in public spaces, without finding shelter or sustenance. Since the last Greek evacuation ship had cast off three days earlier, they found themselves trapped between the quayside and the deep waters of the bay.

When Nicias encountered a bunch of *chettes* coming out of a house with trancelike expressions, as though they had just enjoyed an unspeakable orgasm, he feared the worst. He went inside and found a little girl stuffed in a wardrobe, naked and with her nipples cut. Outraged, he resolved to kill the first one he saw, but when he crossed the brutes in the street he lowered his eyes and walked on past.

Jam-packed and crushed together under the baking sun, massed but isolated, the refugees only stirred when somebody brought water, or some Turks broke into their midst and snatched a child to rape her, or a man to kill him. Fearing a stampede, Nicias tried to stay on the edges of the crowd. But jostled from every side, he was often swept into the center or involuntarily left high and dry on a corner, in a square, or in front of a church.

When the teeming mass disintegrated, it was into smaller swarms, mobile labyrinths that might persist for a minute or an hour. In the midst of the pandemonium, he could hear the creak of branches traversed by the light, the rustle of hands, the friction of fabrics, the scratch of fingers across a chin, a scalp, a shoulder; he could hear the layered voices mounting from hell, while over the cries of women and children the tread of Turkish boots squealed like the hinges of vampire coffins. He could hear breathing, aimless footsteps, the panting of dogs, and even the suffocation in a graying woman's eyes as she pressed an empty cup to a child's lips, with such absorption that they might have been alone in the world—until a passing *chette* struck her between the shoulders with his rifle-butt, and she fell forward to the ground. Nicias perceived the noises, the voices, the groaning near and far as an arrangement of notes

and chords, the variations of a secret concert. Over and above
the ubiquitous, spontaneous wickedness of the Turks, he sensed
the presence of the Divine, the image of God within him.

In Sultan Street a Turkish butcher's shop was open, displaying rumps and ribs and briskets of beef and veal, surrounded
by knives and meat cleavers. The sight of the flayed lambs
affronted him, as though hanging from those meat-hooks were
images of the Lamb of God Himself.

"So many hacked bodies in this city; the whole of Smyrna is
an abattoir," he thought to himself as he skirted the Turkish
quarter. Here Turkish civilians were pushing carts loaded with
horses' heads destined for Anatolia, while Smyrna was starving
to death.

Piercing shrieks came from inside a house. A distraught
woman was hammering on the door, trying to get out. Nicias
climbed in through a hole in the wall. As her legs and hands
were badly burned, he offered to cut away the clothes adhering
to her skin and cover her mouth with a wet cloth. But there was
no water in the house, the doorknob was red hot, and her burns
needed urgent care. Just then an angora cat appeared at the top
of the stairs, looking down toward the open door.

"Ankara kedisi." The snow-white feline with contrasting
eyes, one blue and the other yellow, leaped in sudden panic
through the curtain of fire and smoke, its tail an arching plume
that touched its head.

The roof was falling in. A chair was ablaze. A Turkish regular
was teasing a wounded civilian with the point of his bayonet.
The ultimate sadism of this perpetrator of human sacrifice lay
in tormenting the victim to the very end. Like that *chette* over

there, laughing as he prevented a woman from escaping her burning house.

"Smyrna is like the City of Dreadful Night," said a man in English.

"I've seen dead bodies in every part of town, but the slaughter in the Armenian quarter is the worst." So said the man's companion, an Englishwoman, fanning her face as though the thought of what she had seen made her feel hot.

"I found a child in the street with her breasts shot off. She had blood on her thighs and private parts; it's obvious what the Turks got up to before they killed her."

"Reverend Dobson?" Nicias said.

"The same."

"No one can know what lamb tastes like until he tries it. Just wait for the coming conflagration."

A *chette* was pushing a cart full of gunpowder, kerosene, dynamite, and petroleum towards the Armenian quarter.

"What have you got inside those sacks?" the reverend asked.

"Rice and potatoes for the dying. But they can only open them when they run out of bread."

As he walked through the Greek quarter he heard a scratchy record playing and recognized the melancholy voice of Marika Papagika singing "Smyrna Minore." The words were "If he loves me and I am dreaming, let me never wake up. In the sweetness of dawn, God, just let me die." It was the anguished voice of a Pythian priestess who foresees the collapse of her world and the loss of her beloved.

* * *

On his way to Bayrakli, bordering the Greek cemetery, between the Bournabat road and the train station, Nicias passed St. Augustine's and the Capuchin parish church with his eyes on the dark pine groves and the mountain beyond, on the shadow of the station cast onto the tracks as if no train would ever call there again. Somewhere in the old city he found a concealed passage that led to the ruins of a temple to Athena. There he met a wall with two crumbled capitals, one Aeolic with vertical volutes, the other with horizontal volutes in the Ionic style. The passage divided into two narrow paths. He took the right fork until he came upon a marble kore lying on the ground. The nose and chin had been attacked with a hammer and chisel; the lips were crushed. A veil could be discerned across the face. The eyelids were covered with incisions, and the eyebrows were chipped near the temples. Nearby there was a terracotta mask with red circles around the eyeholes and another of a female face painted white, with orange eyes and red-brown hair, and a statuette representing Potnia Theron, the Mistress of the Animals.

Disappointed at not finding Eurydice, Nicias sat on the floor and slid despite himself into the arms of Morpheus. And there being none to rival the son of Sleep when it comes to flying noiselessly through the shadows and mimicking forms and features, vocal timbres and ways of walking and slipping away, he saw himself in dreams as a contemporary Orpheus in search of Eurydice, the woman bitten by a viper in the grass one day as

she was strolling by a river in Thrace and the peasant Aristaeus
chased after her to rape her.

After her death, Nicias's shadow, Orpheus, went down to
Hades to find her. He coaxed Pluto to send her back, and the
lord of the underworld agreed on one condition: He, Orpheus,
could lead his woman back to the surface but must never turn
to look at her until they were safely out of the kingdom of the
dead. He accepted and set out. He found her among transparent
shades, standing by a bleached cypress. Her eyes were dull, her
body dry with thirst, her hair a tangle.

"Who are you? Where have you come from?" she asked.

"I am Nicias and I have come for you," he whispered into an
ear diaphanous as a listening darkness.

"The sun's light has left my soul."

"Come, I will lead you back to the world of the living." And
the shade followed behind him on light feet, despite the wound
of the viper's fangs. Their steps rang out as they hurried to
reach the mouth of hell before the sun went down. The three-
headed dog was barking at her heels, stretching its three snouts
to sniff her shadow, although she had no shadow. He saw himself as if from outside, crossing the valleys of Hades and the
sacred groves of Persephone's wood; he heard voices of stones
and asphodels, the soar of birds, and many silences. And he was
almost at the gates of Hades, able to glimpse Helios hovering
on golden wings, when he no longer heard her behind him and
turned his head to look and saw her fade, blown back by the
winds to the place she had left.

Nicias awoke pale as death, with his own face again, soaked in
sweat and tears. He wondered why Calliope had told him to

seek Eurydice here, when she knew it was only a dream. Had she done it for the sake of the myth?

In one corner there was a toy house full of rag dolls representing little girls with perforated foreheads, gashed navels, severed legs, pierced chests, split bodies, their lower halves clad in stockings and shoes.

Some held rattles in their broken fingers. Others were made of wood, with articulated joints. Yet others were lying on cardboard cots. Scattered over the floor were tinplate toys: a locomotive, a Pegasus, a watering truck. An ax, a saber, and a gun were made of the same material. Nearby was a Meccano set, a tricycle and a two-wheeled carriage harnessed to a white horse, a boat with two spinning aeroplanes, and a pair of lead Turkish soldiers with their rifles aimed at the head of an Armenian.

> little bodies to mix with
> little bellies to climb on
> little tits to play with
> little mouths to feast on

Had some *chette* scrawled this horrible rhyme on the wall? It was too much. If the thugs had entered the ruins to abuse bodies and vandalize the place, they could not be far off. Nicias made a rapid retreat.

Before sunup on Wednesday, September 13, bands of *chettes* spilled out of the Turkish cemetery and headed for the Armenian quarter. Avoiding the light of the moon, they slunk close to the walls, arms full of cans of gasoline and other flammable liquids which they lobbed into houses, taverns, stores, stations, churches, and hospitals. Like scavenging beasts replete, they lounged contentedly, smoking hashish and drinking raki. Behind them came municipal water trucks stocked with gas and petroleum, and Turkish civilians with torches to ignite the fuel. Buildings began to burn inside.

At dawn Smyrna was beautiful, and a furnace. The fresh autumnal air was enveloped in billowing black smoke. A Greek nurse, seeing three blazes start near the American Collegiate Institute for Girls, spread the word that the Turks were setting the city on fire; Minnie Mills, director of the institute, claimed to have spotted Turkish soldiers throwing petrol cans into homes and shops.

"The purpose of the Turks in setting fire to the city is to obliterate the signs of their atrocities," the nurse maintained. "Wherever their forces go, flames and explosions follow. They burned the bakery down with people inside. Now the whole street is ablaze."

"The fires are deliberate. The Christian districts were torched when the wind was blowing away from the Turkish quarter," said an Armenian woman in a straw hat with blue ribbons. "Their intention is clear: to wipe out *Gavur Izmir*, 'infidel Smyrna.'"

"This is not one great fire, but many fires at once in different zones of the city. Not one smoke cloud, but thousands. Not one but hundreds of hands are stoking the fires. Not one but many militias are to blame. The conflagration first kindled in the Christian neighborhoods is consuming the heart and soul of Smyrna," Nicias observed. "At these signs of genocide, the

Americans, the British, the French, and the Italians are preparing to evacuate their nationals."

"The burning of infidel Smyrna has begun," Nureddin Pasha announced to his staff.

It was after 11 a.m. when Nicias saw a vivid red horse careering down a street in the Armenian quarter. The animal was alight. On incandescent legs it raced as if to overtake itself, flying over the ground. A blazing rider, reins held high, spurred his mount to ever greater efforts, faster, faster, his heart bursting from the fireballs of his eyes. The saddlecloth was smoldering and the saddle was an ember. The Greek horseman shone resplendent with its heat—until the horse lost speed, the flaming legs crumpled, and it crashed to the ground, horse and rider rolled into a single igneous body.

The corpses littering the streets gave off that sweetish odor of eternity characteristic of charred meat. Among the dead were dogs and cats, birds and mice; pets were mixed up with sandals, shoes, hands, bandages, sunshades, scorched frocks. Beyond the indistinctiveness of sex and age, it was impossible to tell whether a skinned jawbone, a detached foot, a stray ear belonged to this body or that. The whole city reeked of fire.

The rank fumes of this open-air crematorium mingled with the stink of burning ruins, rotten eggs, and excrement, the pungency of Turkish meatballs and fried fish and kebabs roasted on the coals of home kitchens and roadside stalls, the whiffs of incense, resin, and perfume compounding the pestilence of open drains, to produce a sickening olfactory overload.

Even the artillery explosions and the screams of doomed men seemed a form of putrefaction.

Nothing. Maimed bodies with purple faces, blackened sockets, claw-like hands; rusty, instantly aged doors hanging askew over a rubble of foundations and walls and window grilles; bronze reproductions of antique statues from the museum that might have been dredged up from a ship that foundered a thousand years ago. Empty bottles and blood-smeared windowpanes, reflecting the same smoked sun. Nothing. A bald old man clutching a letter to Apollo written in Greek, as though the most Greek of all the gods could fly through time and space to save him. Nothing. Women and girls, with alien features they never thought would be theirs, swinging from a lemon tree. Nothing. A general with the ears of a vampire bat had signed the order of wholesale evil, and his troops were carrying out that decree. Nothing. Groans and sighs and whispers wafting from the dead, then nothing. Nothing.

From the old St. Simeon Hospital, named after Simeon the Holy Fool, the sixth-century monk who is the patron of the mentally ill, the lunatics emerged like El Greco apostles with straggling beards, matted hair, and tattered gowns over one shoulder, blessing-cursing everyone they passed with a wave of the right hand. Some, with doughy faces and wandering gazes, beat at the ground with their cloaks; others, uttering stern commands and feline yowls, wrung their hands and rolled their eyes to heaven.

The asylum had been sacked by the *chettes*, and the inmates clambered out through doors and windows and blasted walls. Inside, the younger women had been sheltered from the flames by the high partitions; but, at a signal, the ruffians pounced on them. It was like the story of the Sabine women, except that, in contrast to the Roman myth, the abductors did not want to marry them. They were bent only on rape and murder.

Nicias had a glimpse of the pack's chief, with his goatish face and black fez with the portrait of Mustafa Kemal, as he peered out of a cell window and withdrew, although you could still hear his heavy footsteps and the clangor of his saber and knife. The chief was not concerned with windows: he posted himself at the door, in front of which the maddened women scrambled past. He surveyed their pubescent forms with salacious glee, groping breasts and waists with rough hands, like a slave dealer.

Some Armenian and Greek girls known to Nicias had hidden out in the Simeon Hospital, pretending to be mad. But just as he recognized those young beauties from the Aram, Kasparian, and Berberian families, he began to hear noises from the dormitories of ripping fabric, sobbing women, and panting dogs.

This was happening while other *chettes* encircled the hospital building so as to catch the ones who were trying to get away. With greedy eyes asquint and snapping jaws they proceeded to subdue, strip, and mount them. The sole exception was a melancholy *chette* seated on a bench, puffing hashish.

"Open the gates for there's a great fire in here, and so much flesh around that we will all be consumed!" A patient came out of a room, pulling chains off his wrists and ankles. His long white hair was tangled, and his beard was thick and overgrown. An ash-colored cloak hung off his shoulders.

"Who are you?" Nicias asked him.

"Bartholomaîos, he who was flayed."

"Who is that?"

"The Apostle Bartholomew."

"Why do you want the gates opened?"

"So that the Turks may not bludgeon us to death."

"Respected Galen, unless the doors are opened, we shall perish," boomed another escapee, who called himself James the Elder. He was waving a playing card marked with the Knight of Coins.

"Which gates do you want open?"

"The ones in the wall."

"Why do you have that Knight of Coins, Son of Thunder, glorious gift-bearing apostle?" The man who intercepted him, of medium height, was wearing an animal pelt that had been savaged by dogs.

"Who wants to know?"

"James the Younger."

"Why did you say you wanted them open?"

"To get through the fire."

"Who are you?" a man with shaven head and chin inquired of his companion.

"Thomas."

"Open the secret door in the wall; I must escape to heaven through it; the Turks want to skin me alive," cried Bartholomew.

"All the walls are open."

"Can't you see the sea on the other side?"

"No, you half-wit; on the other side are the Turks; the sea has gone."

"Hush, have you ever been in heaven?"

"Open the doors, I tell you; we're going to die," insisted Bartholomew furiously. "I'm off; this place is full of lunatics."

"Pppff," went Thomas, spitting ashes on the ground.

"That's enough." Naked and flatulent, much like Mad Simeon himself, Bartholomew went down the burning street, dragging a dead dog. The others followed reverently, as though listening to supernatural chants.

Bartholomew-Mad Simeon came to a halt before the blind Greek man, at whose home Nicias had been the day Archbishop Chrysostomos was lynched.

"Learn, my brother, that the water of grace is at once very large and very small; it is widely dispersed but remains gathered; it lasts a long time but is fleeting; I must anoint your eyelids with spittle to cure your blindness."

Nicias went in search of his teacher, Alexis Seferiades. The Turks had set the city library alight, and flames fed on wood and paper were licking at the houses on either side. In the presence of this fire, minor as it was beside the great conflagration devouring Smyrna, Nicias mourned the loss of books, documents, and manuscripts, such as the *Book of Revelation* by St. John Theologos or a woodcut of the Four Horsemen of the Apocalypse, with the number of the Beast assigned to Nero Kemal. After having been preserved from the days of ancient

Greece to those of the very last librarian, whose name was Apollodorus of Ephesus (the same as the author of the *Bibliotheca*), they turned to ashes within minutes.

The truth of poet Heinrich Heine's line in *Almansor* came home to Nicias more powerfully than ever before: "Where they have burned books, they will end up burning human beings."

As the library blazed, its words and images went up in smoke: *Grammata* magazine, Linnaeus's *Om chokladdrycken*, and Antonio Lavedan's *Tratado de los usos, abusos, propiedades y virtudes del Tabaco, Café, Té y Cacao*, with the stamp of Sosias Zacuto, bookseller. Nicias managed to read some phrases in a Bible that was fast combusting: "And the whole earth was of one language, and of one speech . . . And they said, Go to, let us build us a city and a tower, whose top may reach unto heaven; and let us make us a name. . . . Therefore, is the name of it called Babel."

On another page Nicias made out a title in Old Ladino: *Biblia de Ferrara, una tresladasiyon a la lingua djudeo-espanyola del Tanah. Fue publikada en la sivdad italiana de Ferrara en el anyo 1553 para uzo de los sefardies y fue echa por el portuguez Avraam Usque, i el espanyol Yom Tov Atias.*

Before the inferno created by the *chettes*, who had overrun the library building shooting projectiles wrapped in flammable materials, Nicias felt as though he was himself on fire, and that the library cherished by Apollodorus as an ark of books encompassed not only the collection, but his very person. Perhaps that was why he felt no surprise at finding the old man's calcined body, chained to his desk then drenched in gasoline by the Turks. Before him lay a handwritten note that said:

They gouged out the eyes of the two-faced marble Janus. Doubly blind he looked to North and South and saw nothing. The god who confronts blind death with both his faces could not see his own destruction. My sorrow is as ancient and impersonal as the sunset. I know a Greek labyrinth that was trodden by poets, philosophers, historians, geometers, and gods (once men ceased to believe in them). That labyrinth is my own.

The pages cried out, the pictures writhed as though alive, the fire provoked by the liquid fuel scurried over every surface to reach flammable objects. Flames and smoke engulfed the works of Aristotle, Plato, Homer, Herodotus, Heraclitus, Aeschylus, Sophocles, Euripides, and Sappho, with a toneless, constant crackle.

Like a black mask with many contorted mouths and blue-tinged eyes, an image appeared on the smoldering paper, now with an antiquarian cast, now with a sinister patina: the *Whore of Violence*, a work made by the calligrapher-painter Ioannis around 1920. The apocalyptic beast was squatting on the Gulf of Smyrna. The generals, politicians, and businessmen of the West, the military and religious fanatics of Asia Minor: all of them had fornicated with her. All had imbibed the heady wine of her wrath.

As the figure of the harlot was consumed, tongues darted from her navel, igniting the hands that had offered the goblet of death to all those willing to drink. The eyes became red globes, and the crown, surmounted by a crescent moon, betrayed her lineage. Indeed, the fire itself was an offering to the Whore of Violence who was always present in it: ablaze and yet undaunted, ephemeral and yet immortal.

"There are no readers for the poetics of torched paper." With this thought Nicias backed away from the fiery serpent that had reached the nearby bookcase. For along with the bigger fires small ones flourished, nimble and voracious, darting upstairs, dropping from ceilings, racing under the furnishings to light every part of the library. Nor was this all: a Turkish soldier was blowing the flames onto Euclid's *Elements*, and away went the planes, lines, triangles, circles, spheres, and other geometries explored by the Greek sage, considered a necromancer by the Ottomans; the arsonist also destroyed a copy of James Joyce's recently published novel *Ulysses*, suspecting it to concern the Greek hero of that name.

As well as intoxicated by inhaling so much smoke, Nicias felt seared inside, as if his own being was burning along with the library. It pained him especially to make out some letters on a gray page with singed edges and gaping center . . . the letters of a name . . . *E R D C*. . . . And the image in agony seemed to stretch out its arms to encircle, to enkindle him.

Everything was being consumed. Not spared was an engraving of Sabbatai Zevi, the false messiah born in Smyrna in 1623 to a Sephardic family. Above the inscription "The Coronation of Zevi," he was shown enthroned beneath a celestial crown upheld by cherubs. There were some gold coins lying among the cinders of the print. A Turkish beggar scooped them up, saying as he left: "If we managed to burn all this paper, imagine what we'll do to you."

Outside the library Nicias came across a dead Greek girl with a letter in her hand. It was addressed to the Furies.

Smyrna, September 13, 1922

Dear Erinyes,

My parents are dead and they did not deserve to die. Wherever I turn I see evil prevailing, and it seems that here in Asia Minor there is a conspiracy against love.

I ask you to punish those accursed knaves for their wickedness, and to bring down historic vengeance upon their heads.

I know the day will dawn when they come face to face with the ghastly Erinyes, and when they attempt to leave their abode the Furies will bar the way and shut the door, shake out their hair, release their vipers, sink black fangs into their breast, and pursue them throughout the world until the end of time.

Finally, I beg that those who slew my parents and burned young boys and raped young girls may suffer eternal retribution for their horrendous crimes.

Do not forget, Erinyes, to shroud their souls.

Thus implores you,

Little Sappho

* * *

George Ward Price, the *Daily Mail* correspondent, sent a cable in the early hours that described what he was witnessing from the deck of HMS *Iron Duke*:

> Smyrna has been practically destroyed by a gigantic fire. . . .
> What I see . . . is an unbroken wall of fire, two miles long, in
> which twenty distinct volcanoes of raging flame are throwing
> up jagged, writhing tongues to a height of a hundred feet. All
> Smyrna's rich warehouses, business-buildings and European
> residences are burning like furious torches. From this
> intensely glowing mass of yellow, orange and crimson fire
> pour up thick, clotted coils of oily black smoke that hide the
> moon at its zenith. . . . many thousands of refugees [are]
> huddled on the narrow quay, between the advancing fiery
> death behind and the deep water in front, [and there] comes
> continuously such frantic screaming of sheer terror as can be
> heard miles away. . . . Picture a constant projection into a red-
> hot sky of gigantic incandescent balloons, burning oil spots in
> the Aegean, the air filled with nauseous smell, while parching
> clouds, cinders and sparks drift across us—and you can but
> have a glimmering of the scene of appalling and majestic
> destruction which we are watching.[6]

While Ward Price was telegraphing his report, the ship's officers followed the progress of the fire and the massacre in the
harbor through their field glasses. At last, the journalist fell
silent, breathing deeply as if short of air, as if his eyes could

[6] Giles Milton, *Paradise Lost: Smyrna 1922: The Destruction of a Christian City in the Islamic World* (London: Sceptre/Hodder & Stoughton,
2009), 321–325.

take in no more of the catastrophic scene and his words had dried up, incapable of depicting horror any further.

"You're not allowed on board. Leave the ship immediately, or be forcibly removed and handed over to the Turks." Two marines with their guns trained on Nicias sent him in a lighter back to shore, where thousands of people were jostling perilously close to the edge, at constant risk of being pitched into the sea.

Percy Hadkinson, one of the last Englishmen to board a lighter ferrying British nationals to a battleship, vowed to write a letter to the British high commissioner in Constantinople, informing him of everything he had seen that night. He wrote, "If Your Excellency could only have heard the cries for help and seen defenseless women and children unmercifully shot down or rushed into the sea to be drowned like rats, or back into the flames to be burned to death, you would fully have realised the horror and extreme gravity of the situation."[7]

The testimony of a Joseph M. was gathered by René Puaux, correspondent of *Le Temps*: "At four o'clock in the afternoon, the commanding officer of the French destroyer *Tonkinois* asked me to accompany him to the police station in order to fetch a police officer to check the passports of those who were queuing to embark on the *Phrygie*. . . . Boarding began straight away. The crowd was enormous. Two naval officers from the *Tonkinois*, with some of their sailors, and a Turkish officer with his own men, supervised the embarkation of the refugees. . . . An Armenian man under French protection was run through

---

[7] Ibid., 318.

with a bayonet before our eyes. . . . A huge crowd of Christians had gathered in front of the consulate, calling for the protection of France. The Turkish officer wanted to push them back towards the flames. The *Tonkinois* officers opposed him. A violent altercation ensued. The Turk, egged on by the Ottoman hordes seeking an excuse to slaughter Christians, drew his revolver and shot the two French officers dead. A skirmish and fusillade ensued. . . . Turkish civilians and the Turkish patrol fired into the crowd of refugees and French sailors. American troops intervened, beat back the Turks, and restored order."[8]

It was then that Nureddin Pasha appeared on the balcony of the hotel which was now the Turkish headquarters, to watch the running people engulfed in flames.

From the slopes of Mount Pagus Nicias contemplated the fiery annihilation of Smyrna, the smoky plumes uniting into black monsters that rose up from buildings and bodies as if from a single combustible tissue. The Greek, Armenian, and European neighborhoods were burning to the ground, while the Turkish quarter, spared by the Kemalist troops, appeared intact.

Nicias could hear the crackle of that many-headed snake of flame as it wound through the streets, sliding under doors, breaking through walls, and resting on rooftops as though revived by the surrounding inferno; he heard the roar of fireballs devouring edifices inside and out. As well as the individual stories of thousands of people, centuries of civilization were being wiped out before his eyes. He, as his own ghost, knew

---

[8] René Puaux, *La Mort de Smyrne* (Paris: Revue des Balkans, 1922), 24–25.

that he would never now be able to divide his being from the razed city—as though man and landscape were the same thing, the same ruins.

"There is more fire here than in hell," he thought, as smoke effaced the horizon, high roofs caved in on lower ones, and the crimson-orange-bluish sky projected dancing demons on the Quay.

To the west, the conflagration had overtaken the Quay, from Bella Vista as far as the Customs House. To the south it grazed the Basmahane railway station. To the east it encompassed the Aydin line, but the tobacco factory was untouched. To the north it had gained Hadji Pasha and Massurdi Streets.

Among the buildings that had burned were the Splendid, Smyrna Palace, Grand Hotel Kramer Palace, Huck and Aegean Sea hotels; the Oriental Carpet Manufacturers; social centers including the Cercle de Smyrne, the Country Club, the Greek Club, and the Sporting Club; almost every Greek and Armenian Orthodox church; the YMCA; the stores along Frank Street and the waterfront; and the American Girls' School. The *chettes* fed the pyres, unhindered by any Turkish authority. The goal: to cremate the dead and erase all traces of their crime.

Boulevards, pharmacies, cinemas, warehouses, post offices, banks, hospitals—all were ravaged. Their entrails spewed thick clouds of smoke and their frames resembled skeletons. Fiery worms gobbled everything in their path. Not only men but also their beasts—dogs, cats, parakeets, horses—the creatures that found themselves trapped like their masters in homes and streets.

Bent over the balconies of hotels or banks, the *chettes* laughed at the people blundering desperately to and fro through the blazing labyrinth. Even more entertaining was to see a flame-wrapped figure plummet from an upper floor. An otherworldly incandescence bathed the city of this world. Ravenous tongues and black smoke sprang from doorways and windows. A diabolical plan was being carried out in Smyrna: to put the Christian population to death by fire.

From Mount Pagus Nicias looked across at Mount Yamanlar, near whose summit lay the volcanic crater called Karagöl, "black lake," the site where Tantalus is held to be buried. According to the legend, this ruler was punished for a terrible crime by being immersed in the lake up to his chin, with a stone dangling above, able to see fruit trees growing on the nearby shores. But when the mythical founder of Smyrna tried to drink, the waters drained away around him; and when he sought to pick the fruits within his reach, they were blown by the wind from his grasp. "That will be the mythological punishment of Kemal for having set the whole city and its people on fire," Nicias said to himself.

The September dusk beyond the pines glowed clear. The waters of the gulf mirrored a cinder-laden sky. Then the panorama was veiled by thousands of starlings, swirling over the city in fright at the fire that had destroyed their nesting places.

As if threaded on a long ribbon of clamorous wings, the birds were tossed by the currents into dark whirlpools and fractured circles. The flames, the shooting, the explosions had set them wildly soaring.

Masters of empty space, they wheeled and swerved, tracing

spirals, forming into spheres and planes and zigzag clouds, while a marble faun way down below observed their airy climb.

Open *O*'s, plunging *L*'s, whistling *S*'s, neurotic *R*'s, the interfaces of song and shadow, of the permanent and the passing, the mobile and the oblivious, wove through their eerie flight, from end to end of the sky, drawing whimsical blotches, splintered skeletons, undulating forms that met and fell apart into smaller forms, spinning vertiginously, tearing to pieces and converging once more.

They were escaping from what was here to return to the point of departure. For a while, taking off again, they teemed over plazas, rooftops, bell towers, and craggy outcrops. Until the whole flock receded into the ashen sky like a solitary *S*, winging over the fire towards the sea.

A macabre resplendence floated over the port, which had lost its night to the flames. Within this brazier a thousand incandescent virgins writhed in agony.

"Nureddin Pasha's arsonists are thrusting petrol-soaked rugs through windows to feed the flames, while their bastard sons have sealed off the Armenian quarter to prevent anyone from going in or out," said an Armenian named Aram as he came down a burning staircase, talking to himself like a madman. "But I saw some *chettes* sneak past the cordon so as to rape men's daughters. And if by chance a woman appears, a mature vine, a rabble of Turkish scum descends on her with lust written on their faces. Get away, get away, for death is contagious."

Nobody fought the fires. Nobody slept. The sanitary conditions were appalling. The city was an encampment and a crematorium. People ran past, beating at the flames on their clothes. Nicias thought that if he could make it to the dock he would jump into the sea.

"Mother Zero, Mother Steel, Mother Crow, Mother Zero. The shortest, simplest route to suicide is to stop in front of a drunken Turk," muttered Aram in Ladino. But when he glimpsed, through the window of a torched house, a young woman with blisters all over her suppurating, inflamed skin, and saw her father, an elderly man with the face of a faun, searching the street for a weapon to kill himself, he fell silent.

"What's your name?" asked Nicias of a young Greek girl, tanned more by fire than by the sun.

"Hermione," she whispered, as if not wanting anybody else to hear it.

"I would make love to you, but now I can do no more than look," he confessed before her body: from behind a little frog, from the front a little goddess. "There's such tenderness in your face, you transmit such rapture in living, that I hope with all my heart you find a boat to take you away," he was saying, when the crowd came between them and a coarse man stood where she had been.

"*Taci, maladetto lupo! Consuma dentro te con la tua rabbia.*" An Italian man was hurling Dante's words against Mustafa Kemal. He was hallucinating the Turkish general in a group of ruffians, pointing at him with his finger.

There was no escape. The fire raged through the city. Women and children squealed like animals in terror. Crowds rushed frantically from the French consulate to the American consulate, both in flames, from shopping arcades to hotel lobbies, from the main square to the Point, hunting for a way out. People overran the quays, flocked to the station at the Caravan Bridge, tried to hide their daughters in open graves or the abandoned villas of Bournabat and Boudja. They poured past the remains of the church of Agios Ioannis, past the American Theater and the imposing French government building, past the Customs House and the Passport Office, past the foreign clubs. In the smoldering embers of every place they sought shelter, protection, a chance for escape, but all they found was rebuff, severed communications, and Turkish army trucks circulating through Smyrna as they pleased.

Everything ablaze. Everywhere a furnace. No matter that sea breezes kept the ground from becoming a griddle: the refugees were set to perish in this pyre, their scorched garments kindling into one-man fires.

Behind the American consulate a band of flame mounted the walls until it found the flag, which caught alight, snapping in the wind, before vanishing behind gusts of smoke.

Nicias was hungry and thirsty, for he had hardly eaten since the rout of the Greek army, and indeed since he had enlisted in its ranks. And when he had slept it had been on the floor, or standing up, or sitting on a rock, or leaning against a wall, once allowing himself to dream that he was Perseus the invisible— guided by Hermes and Athena, with Hades's helmet on his head—who saw others at leisure, unseen by all. And turning his bronze shield to show the Turkish Medusa to herself, he cut off her head.

* * *

The *chettes* congregated in the main square, swarmed up Frank Street; they rampaged from the Konak and the Turkish quarter on foot and on horseback; they appeared behind trees or between the tombs in the Greek and Armenian cemeteries; they crouched under bushes, by waysides and in blackened fields; they hid in public transport vehicles, in old automobiles, in toilets; they scrambled from the roofs of ruined houses, grabbed hold of women cowering in attics or under beds or inside chests; they loitered on corners, irrupted from burned-out hotel rooms and through the red-hot doors of churches and hospitals; they set fire to icons and crosses, blockaded roads, took control of bridges, screened the access to train stations; they scoured Mount Pagus, Mount Yamanlar, the black lake, Bournabat, Boudja, Paradise; they passed messages and herded captives; they seemed ubiquitous and frenziedly active; directed by the officers of the regular army, they harried the Christians with bayonets, whips, and daggers; they showed no mercy, murdering, raping, and robbing stores and homes at whim, as well as stealing trifles from those who were already destitute.

"Help." A small girl detached herself from the crowd, clutching her treasure: a burning doll.

"Give her to me," called a man who may have been her father.

"No!" piped the child in the torn dress. As if it were a physical extension of herself, she wouldn't let go of her doll even as the fire bit fiercely into it. She was determined to burn with it as though the two formed one person, a single flammable material.

The child reached Nicias with her hair, chest, and hands on fire. She fell forward, tightly hugging her play double, until her legs came away from her trunk like those of a dismembered toy.

"Every Armenian will be run to ground and killed, wherever he may be. Even Turkish adolescents will join the sport." So the crowd was warned by Captain Arthur Hepburn, chief of staff of the American Naval Detachment.

"Armenians are not the only ones who must beware; so must the Greeks. Men sleeping in the open air with their belongings must be prepared, even hopelessly, to defend their womenfolk," added the American sergeant next to him.

"Now that the Turks are running out of things to steal, they're getting more aggressive. They can come down like a pack of wolves on refugees anywhere, to snatch their daughters, wives, and sisters," Captain Hepburn said.

"How is it that Mustafa Kemal does not show his face or speak?" Bartholomew asked. "It's because Bartholomaîos tied up his tongue with red-hot chains and he doesn't dare say a word on pain of turning into a statue of fire."

Disconcerted by this outlandish figure, Hepburn and the sergeant did not reply.

Bartholomew went on: "As you will see, I can appear and disappear as I please, and should I vanish in the next second, don't ask after me; I won't be seen again."

Just then the Greeks noticed a ship approaching, and they surged forward. Although they knew the captain had orders not to pick up anyone, they stampeded onto the pier. Bartholomew went with them, swallowed up by the dense human mass.

* * *

From the bridges of their battleships and destroyers, Allied officers watched through raised binoculars as the Turks continued their slaughter of men, women, and children unimpeded.

The USS *Lawrence*, the *Winona*, and the *Edsall* had been dispatched to the Gulf of Smyrna to protect the lives and property of Americans, and to evacuate Greek refugees from the Turkish-occupied zones of Asia Minor. Admiral Sir Osmond de Beauvoir Brock, commander aboard the British dreadnought HMS *Iron Duke*, ignored the inferno being endured by the Christians on the docks: he not only maintained his customary etiquette, making the officers attend dinner in white mess jackets, but he also ordered the ship's band to play some tunes. But when these failed to block out the shrieks of women and children being burned alive, he had the stewards put *Pagliacci* on the phonograph, so that Enrico Caruso's guffaws in the aria *"Vesti la giubba . . . Ridi, Pagliaccio"* mingled with the victims' cries. Admiral Brock had assured Nureddin Pasha of "Great Britain's absolute neutrality," and specified that Britain would not participate in the rescue of Greek and Armenian civilians.

After dinner, Major Arthur Maxwell, focusing his field glasses on the quays, observed the Turks dousing the refugees with pails of burning fuel. Finally, well after midnight, the admiral was persuaded to join in the rescue, and thousands of Greeks and Armenians were taken on board many of the ships in the harbor.

The peak of infamy was reached by Rear Admiral Mark Bristol, the US high commissioner to the Ottoman Empire and commander of US Navy ships in Turkish waters, who forbade his men to succor the Christians—Armenians and Greeks, whom he loathed—preferring to protect and promote Standard Oil and other American business interests with the Turks.

"The horror, the horror." The sandwich man from the Smyrna Theater, wrapped in flames, stumbled through the panicked scene on the waterfront.

The inescapable smell of roasted flesh grew more nauseating every minute, and by nightfall the situation had so deteriorated that the bulk of refugees found themselves trapped in the harbor. Kemal's men, not satisfied by the hell they had created, continued tearing girls from their parents' arms to be raped in front of them, killing unarmed men, and throwing incendiary bombs into the crowd. The flames that towered ever taller and broader were consuming homes, hotels, churches, hospitals, and consulates; and many petrified children, unable to respond to their mothers' hysterical calls, were too traumatized to speak at all.

Borne up at the heart of the crowd, Nicias's feet did not touch the ground, and the fierce heat seared his nostrils. Jostled and buffeted, amid the groaning of people in flames or swept towards the edge of the Quay, he struggled not to fall in while fighting his way toward a ship that was itself retreating from the dock, to avoid being reached by either the fire or the mob.

"Nicias?" A woman in a torn peplum called out behind him. Her lovely breasts were wounded, breasts he once compared to the golden apples of the Hesperides. He used to say, "Calliope, those apples don't reside in Libya, as some mythomaniacs would have it, but on the atlas of my friend's body. The hundred-headed dragon himself would lack the tongues to praise them."

"Help me," she stammered. Blood trickled from her bosom. "I've been tortured. The Turks staged a fake execution. They blindfolded me at dawn and set me in front of a squad that fired into the wall."

"Is there anything I can do?"

"I'm looking for my daughter, Artemis; she has disappeared from Smyrna. I just hope she turns up on the islands. Help me."

"Where is Eurydice. Do you know?"

"She's hiding somewhere in the Greek quarter. To find her in this crowd would be impossible."

"She has to come with me."

"To her death?"

"I'm not leaving here alone."

"Forget her; she's married to another man."

"You're lying, to make me desert her."

"Didn't she tell you she has a daughter with him?"

"No, she did not."

"So now you know."

"Why didn't she wait for me?"

"She did. She waited years. But when she didn't hear from you she thought you'd been killed in battle . . . or that you'd gone into exile, and would not be coming back."

"This man she lives with, who is he?"

"His name doesn't matter."

"Where did he come from?"

"He came from Istanbul."

"What does he do?"

"He works in the underground."

"How did she meet him?"

"On secret operations. Twice he saved her life. Go on now, or it'll be too late."

"I'm not leaving."

"You've changed."

"I haven't; the death of the city has transformed me. Wherever I go, I shall never be the same again."

"Leave."

"The phoenix of joy will never resurrect in this murdered city. The Turkish backwater that succeeds it will contain nothing but amnesia and mediocrity."

"Go now, the vampire men are approaching. "

"She has to come with me."

"Adieu." She stepped into the throng like a sleepwalker.

"Calliope!" He tried to stop her, but she was lost in the multitude. In her place appeared the apostles of the old Simeon Hospital with singed beards, robes, and hair. Some wore cloaks draped over one shoulder and were blessing the refugees. Others struck the ground with their staves, and cursed the Turks.

James the Younger lifted his hands to heaven.

"Throw open the city gates for there is a very great fire. If they are not opened the Turks are going to roast us alive. So commands Bartholomaîos, he who holds back the waters."

The last named stopped in front of Nicias. His hair was the color of ashes.

James the Elder, still brandishing his playing card, said, "Respected Galen, if the gates are not opened the Turks will bludgeon us to death."

"What gates are you after opening, Son of Thunder?" James the Younger inquired, with a wild look in his eye. "But first tell me, why do you still have that Knight of Coins?"

"Open up. The Turks want my skin!" cried Andrew.

"Why do you want the gates opened?"

"Because beyond lies the sea."

"Pppff," went Thaddeus, coughing up cinders.

"Learn, my brother, that the water of grace is at once very large and very small; it is widely dispersed but remains gathered; it lasts a long time in one place, but is fleeting; to cure the Turks of their blindness, I must anoint their eyelids with spittle."

Dragging the charred carcass of the dog, Bartholomew moved towards the Turkish soldiers. Their guns were aiming at him but did not fire as he went by, intoning a Byzantine chant in so deep a voice that the vocal monody seemed to rise from inward caverns. With the crepitation of flames for its sole accompaniment, the "Troparion of the Resurrection" seemed to become part of the city's agony as Bartholomew led his disciples into a blazing hotel, singing:

> Angelic hosts appeared above thy tomb
> To protect, Maria Theotokos, thy immaculate body.
> In depths of Hades the guards did perish
> Burned by flames of ice within.
> O thou who didst rise from the dead
> O thou who wert transfigured by fire
> Glory be to Thee.

"Come and look," an English seaman hollered. "The Turks are burning the refugees alive by throwing buckets of petrol over them, and if any cling on to the boats they hack off their arms so that they fall back into the sea."

"If the devil had a nationality it would be Turkish, and if he had a name it would be Mustafa Kemal," said the soliloquizing Armenian as he went by.

"Everyone wants to escape from the flames." A man whose voice was hoarse with smoke was being shoved left and right by the crowd. "But I will enter my blazing body, I will be consumed in my fire."

"Professor Seferiades," Nicias exclaimed.

"The fire, the fire!" cried the man, who was wearing a scarlet tunic and a single bronze sandal. "Perfidious gods who betray the men who love you, hermaphrodite gods who lay skeletons on the couch of Eros. Heraclitus knew the truth: This world-order, the same of all, no god nor man did create, but it ever was and is and will be: ever living fire, kindling in measures and being quenched in measures."

Seferiades vaulted the railings and, like Empedocles casting himself into the crater of Mount Etna, plunged into a bonfire. His clothes and body caught alight, and robed in flames he dwindled to nothing on his own pyre.

Save for the Turkish and Jewish quarters, the whole of Smyrna was fire and ashes, and the scramble to escape redoubled. Refugees crawled out of houses, stores, churches, and hideaways and made for the quays, limping, injured, blinded, deafened, stunned and stupefied, pushed helplessly this way and that,

with a sick relative, an old man, or a child in their arms. The
waterfront was so packed with humanity that it was hard to
move an inch. The air smothered faces and bodies like a hot
cloth; clouds of acrid, stinging smoke enveloped the port, and
the shrieks of half a million people maddened by fear rever-
berated for miles over the din of explosions, collapsing buildings, and machine-gun volleys. The Christian population,
assailed by the fire and the Turkish weapons, saw no end to
their suffering. Their despair increased whenever a boat was
seen to pull away, crammed with refugees, leaving them behind
in hell.

The panic was contagious. The screams of women and children could be heard for miles around like the howling of a
thousand-headed beast. Although one multitude was already
too many, other multitudes poured relentlessly into the same
space. Their one purpose was to board a ship or lighter bound
for the Greek islands, no matter if it were so overloaded it
would capsize. Otherwise, there were three options: to surren-
der to the flames, to jump into the deep waters of the gulf, or to
be gunned down by the Turks. And one more possibility: the
individual impulse of ultimate black humor that would lead a
man to take his own life.

But the picture of hell offered by the dark boiling of the sky
and the flashes of ghastly brilliance rising from the ground
mounted to crescendos of despair when the vessels anchored by
the Quay began to withdraw from the fire zone, with people
clinging to their sides, and a destroyer began to steam away.
That was when the hundreds of thousands of refugees who
found themselves trapped in the monstrous bonfire turned into

"a solid mass of desperate humanity," in the words of Captain Arthur Hepburn.

There could be no doubt about it: the city that for centuries had withstood every onslaught, from earthquakes to conquests by the likes of Tamburlaine, was being erased from the map by fire. "Turkey for the Turks," in the nationalist rhetoric of Mustafa Kemal, would make of it a ruined backwater, and even streets and neighborhoods would be renamed so as to efface every last sign of its historic past. The Megali Idea had turned to ashes; the thousands-year-old Greek presence on the Eastern coast of the Aegean Sea was at an end.

Nicias read a proclamation that had been posted around the city on September 16.

1. All Greek and Armenian males between the ages of 18 and 45 who are found in places that have been freed by our army, as well as those Greeks and Armenians brought by the Greek army to the coast for evacuation and abandoned as a result of our army's unstoppable advance, must henceforth consider themselves prisoners of war. They will be held as prisoners until the end of hostilities. This measure is taken because they took up arms against the Fatherland, because they trained in the enemy army, because they have set fire to towns and villages and committed unprecedented atrocities against the peaceful population, and to prevent them from swelling the ranks of the enemy army.

2. Those who are not subject to the preceding provision, and

all Smyrnean families or Greek and Armenian refugees, have until September 30 to emigrate. Once the deadline is passed, those who have not left the country and are deemed a potential threat to the security of the army and to public order will be conducted out of the war zone.

3. The Great National Assembly having taken measures to cleanse the country of the debris of the Greek army and to annihilate the enemy's destructive organizations, all inhabitants, without distinction of race or religion, should return to their homes and resume their peaceful activities.

The Commander of the Army

General Nureddin

He understood this to mean that women, children, and old men would be permitted to leave before the deadline, and that their men would be taken East to be slaughtered.

Nicias knew that the Turkish authorities had been fomenting a widespread boycott of Ottoman-Greek interests, and pasting notices in schools and mosques that incited the Muslim population to hound and kill their Christian neighbors.

One poster put up in the Turkish quarter read:

THE GREEKS ARE RAPING OUR WOMEN.
WE CALL UPON EVERY TURK TO RAPE THE
   GREEK WOMEN.
LONG LIVE DEATH!

* * *

Under the sun and the rain, ankle-deep in water and mud, on their way to leaving life behind, the day's deportees filed past Nicias.

"They do not know the way." Goya's etching of prisoners roped together at the neck, shuffling hunched and despairing towards exile, could well have illustrated the scene. But the difference between Goya's captives and the Greek and Armenian deportees was that the latter were civilian victims of the hellish Turkish prison system. He had heard that years earlier, when the Armenians were slaughtered, the women were driven to the Magnesia region in threes, naked, fated to be raped and hung from the trees. Children from three to seven years old had stumbled towards execution. Flushed from their homes or hiding places or shelters with nothing but the clothes they had on, men and women became links in the long chain of death. On the road to deportation in Kharput or somber Anatolia, the scarecrows and the scared had seemed to belong to the same grisly club: the first as predators, the second as prey.

From the Caravan Bridge, Nicias now watched the "labor teams" cross the wrecked city under the lash and the rifle butt. They were chivvied up the steep paths in the knowledge of having lost dominion over their bodies, knowing too that their cruel overseers would not hesitate to use barbed-wire scourges and bayonets on them, to withhold food and water and deny medicine to the sick. Sooner rather than later, therefore, these thousands of Greeks and Armenians of an age to die would succumb to typhus, cold, or fatigue.

Bound and herded, they were harassed by vicious, fanatical, rutting guards whose sole aim was to exhaust and exterminate them. Or, more speedily, to execute them five by five; to thoroughly demoralize them by forcing them to witness the abuse of their wives and daughters. Driven like cattle to the Turkish quarter, to the army barracks where thousands like them were already corralled in filthy yards, the wretches looked at the ground. Nicias resolved at once to take his own life rather than be captured by the *chettes*, sadistic fiends straight out of a circle of Dante's *Inferno*, primitive brigands Mustafa Kemal had called up from the depths of backward Anatolia.

"Hundreds of prisoners were sprawled on the sand under the baking sun," an Armenian would say later on board ship. Hovakim Uregian had survived a flogging by the *chettes*. He went on: "They were in rags, without hats or shoes. Destitute. The Turks had robbed them of everything."

Elsewhere in the tightly packed group, a mother's bony hand came down gently on her child's head, protectively, as if in adversity the hand moved of its own accord in a gesture of blessing rather than succor.

"Where is your fez with the portrait of Mustafa Kemal?" demanded a Turkish soldier, cocking his rifle.

"My fez?"

"You will be deported to Magnesia. You won't be alone; five thousand Greeks will go with you. Fewer than that will arrive, because at every stretch of the way the guards will do some thinning out. With any luck, you'll make it but in poor shape."

"Water," Nicias pleaded.

"You can dig for it in dried-up wells."

"My lips are cracked."

"You can drink river water sweetened by rotting flesh."

"Will I reach Magnesia alive?"

"If you're not sold into slavery before."

The soldier beckoned to an officer who was rounding up Greek youths for deportation and Armenian girls for sex. Nicias went cold. At that moment a panic-stricken crowd burst into the street and overwhelmed them. He took advantage of the commotion to escape.

The beds of death, the stones of the way.

In response to their efforts, on September 22 Rev. Asa K. Jennings, who had only arrived in Smyrna in August to work at the YMCA, and Halsey Powell, commander of the USS *Edsall*, obtained permission from Nureddin to allow Greek merchant ships to enter the harbor at Smyrna, although not under their own flag and without tying up at the Quay, to begin the evacuation of refugees. The first Greek ships steamed in two days later. Even then, however, the Turkish soldiers did their best to prevent people going aboard, grabbing their belongings and beating or killing any who resisted. The crews of Allied ships had listened all night long to the cries of terrified little girls and men being mown down.

"Women and children only; men keep back, get back!"

The seamen fought to restrain the human avalanche unfurling over the gangways, now that the Turks were combing the crowd for males aged between fifteen and sixty to keep as prisoners. Mustafa Kemal had decreed that from the first of October, all refugees would be deported to Central Anatolia.

"Look, a horse, a horse on fire!" shouted a mariner who was helping winch up an anchor. Every gaze turned toward the flaming beast galloping wildly through the crowd, trampling on women and children until, like a fabulous creature made of heat and light, it threw itself into the sea.

Elbowing his way through the refugees massed on the Quay, Nicias managed to convince the Turkish guards that he was French, as he had excelled in the language at high school, and to board the *Zakynthos*, but his heart plummeted when he saw Eurydice on the pier, with a baby in her arms. She was preceded by a man holding a black suitcase who looked like the man in black he had seen at the railway station, the day of the asses. Behind them ran a girl of about eight years old.

"Eurydice!" The man spun to warn her just as they reached a boat, but a guard stabbed her in the ankle, and she sank to the ground.

"Eurydice!" Nicias cried out as he saw she didn't move, and the man was being shot by the Turks, and the child was wresting the baby from her mother's arms and braving the flames and the bullets and at last being helped onto a ship by a sailor.

The Turks quickly tossed Eurydice's body into the flames, while the man dragged himself to the edge and toppled into the bay.

For the eternity of an instant Nicias watched the head of this unknown Orpheus bobbing on the water, unable to sink, buoyed by the corpses beneath him. Of Eurydice he would preserve the image of a yellow outline fingered by the sunbeams of an uncanny dawn. Strange to say, beyond this Orpheus, beyond this Eurydice, the sun flared like a liquid flower on the sea.

"No more passengers. Everyone on deck," cried a Greek mariner on the *Zakynthos*, and the *Ismini*, the *Matheos*, the *Thraki*, the *Atromitos*, the *Peneos*, and the *Byzantion*, packed with passengers, also began to move.

Escaping aboard the *Simpson* ten days earlier, the American consul in Smyrna, George Horton, would write:

> As the destroyer moved away from the fearful scene and darkness descended, the flames, raging now over a vast area, grew brighter and brighter, presenting a scene of awful and sinister beauty . . . nothing was lacking in the way of atrocity, lust, cruelty and all that fury of human passion which, given their full play, degrade the human race to a level lower than the vilest and cruelest of beasts. . . . One of the keenest impressions which I brought away with me from Smyrna was a feeling of shame that I belonged to the human race.[9]

"Bid Smyrna farewell, for it has betrayed you; bid farewell to the city you will never see again, although its relics remain, because the Smyrna you knew will not return; your Smyrna has been expunged from the geography of being. Asia Minor has died within you." Nicias's head rang with the words spoken by Seferiades while packs of Turkish boys were diving into the water to saw with knives and razors at the fingers, wrists, ears, and necks of the dead whose jewelry they coveted, their mouths and noses covered with a rag so as not to smell the rotting bodies.

---

[9] Horton, *Blight of Asia*, 152–153.

Nicias stood fast against his Thanatos, that figure of the Lord of the Dead camouflaged in black drapes of restless water, who seemed to pull the survivors of the genocide into the deeps of the sea of history to drown them in the oblivion of the present.

"Away," my father said quietly to himself, as the *Zakynthos* churned through the dead of the Levantine city. Leaning on the ship's rail he grieved for the unspeakable, infernal horror the Turks had created during those September days in 1922. Little by little, amid a thick sepulchral pall and a sickening odor of burned flesh, he saw the fire darken heaven and earth and the city disappear.

HISTORICAL IMAGES

SOUVENIR DE SMYRNE.   Vue du Quartier Armenien.

Postcard showing the Armenian quarter of Smyrna
at the beginning of the twentieth century.
AGMI Collection.

SMYRNE

Echelle
500 T
0   1 K

GOLFE DE S... M...

Feu Rouge

Feu Vert

Spen...

PORT

Douane

Fort
St Pierre

de
l'hôpital

QUARTIER

Hopit...
Grec

Place
d'Armes   Konak

Port Ferm...

Fontaine

BAZARS

De Kara-Tach
Cimetière Juif

Prisons

Odéon

QUARTIER JUIF

Hopital
Juif

Aïob-Mahallé

Agora

Tchoukour-...

Portes Éphésiennes

Kara Gumbroü

Cimetières Turcs

QUARTIER TUR...

Portes de Magn...

Baracks

Enceinte

Théâtre

Silvr...
12

Stade
Antique

Château

2
9

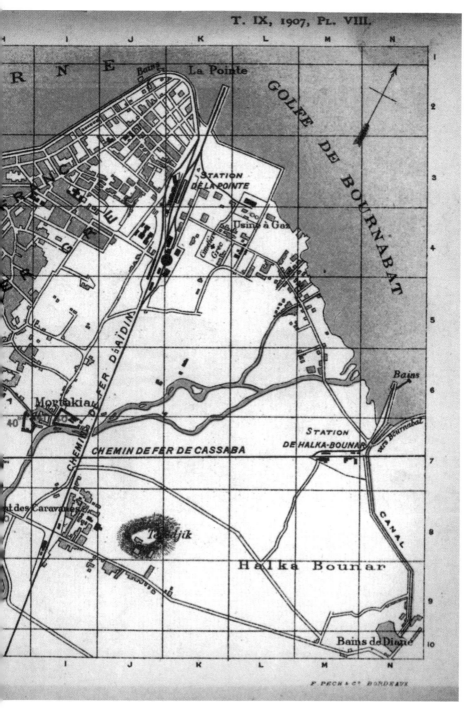

Map of the city of Smyrna drawn by Aristote Fontrier,
published in *Revue des études anciennes*, September 1907.

An everyday scene on the waterfront, ca. 1920.

View of Smyrna from the outskirts, February 1, 1921.
© Frederick Simpich/National Geographic Society/Corbis.

View of the main port of Smyrna, February 1, 1921.
© Frederick Simpich/National Geographic Society/Corbis.

A street scene in the commercial zone, destroyed by the fire along with the
Armenian and European quarters and the American consulate, August 15, 1922.
© Underwood & Underwood/Corbis.

Mustafa Kemal, president of the Turkish Grand National Assembly, and his Smyrnean wife, Latifa Hanouz, ca. 1922. © Bettmann/Corbis.

Josefina Fuentes, the Mexican wife of Nicias Aridjis, in Contepec, Michoacán, Mexico, ca. 1927. Courtesy of the author.

Nicias Aridjis, ca. 1922. Courtesy of the author.

Smyrna after the fire. *New York Times* photograph, September 1922.

The United States consulate after the fire, September 1922.

Armenian and Greek prisoners on their way to exile, Smyrna,
September 1922. AGMI Collection.

Christians afloat, rescued from the Kemalist atrocities,
September 1922. AGMI Collection.

Smyrna harbor crowded with terrified refugees,
September 1922. AGMI Collection.

Smoke billowing from buildings on Smyrna's coast,
September 1922. AGMI Collection.

The Passport Office destroyed by fire, September 1922.
AGMI Collection.

The Great Fire of Smyrna, September 1922.
AGMI Collection.

Smyrnean Greeks attempting to board a ship to escape
from Turkish troops, September 1, 1922.
© Hulton-Deutsch Collection/Corbis.

Greek cavalry charging Turkish forces on the outskirts of Smyrna in an
attempt to cover the retreat of their own troops, September 16, 1922.

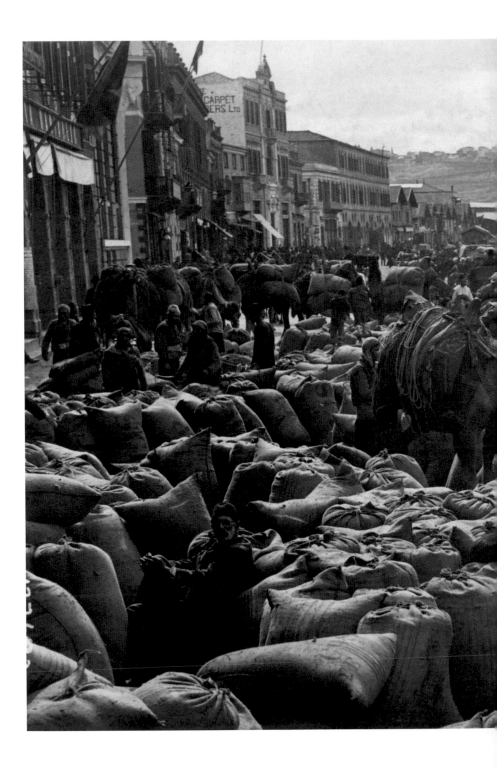

View of the fig market by the harbor, ca. 1922.
© Underwood & Underwood/Corbis.

Greek light artillery ready to continue the fight
against the Turks, September 18, 1922.
© Bettmann/Corbis.

The Turkish population of Smyrna welcomes Mustafa Kemal into
the city, February 19, 1923.
© Bettmann/Corbis.

USS *Lawrence*, ca. 1925.
Courtesy of Naval History and Heritage Command.

USS *Simpson*, ca. 1925.
Courtesy of Naval History and Heritage Command.

Litchfield, ca. 1930.
Courtesy of Naval History and Heritage Command.

Edsall, ca. 1930.
Courtesy of Naval History and Heritage Command.

Nicias Aridjis in his fig orchard at Contepec, Michoacán, Mexico, ca. 1982.
Courtesy of the author.

Postscript

On reaching Athens Nicias obtained his discharge from the War and Naval Secretariat, and learned that General Georgios Hatzianestis had been shot for high treason. Nicias went to Volos to seek out his parents, Theologos and Penelope, among the refugees from Asia Minor. An acquaintance told him that they were in Brussels with his brother Niarchos, but his brother Kostas and his uncle Aristides had been murdered by the Turks. Nicias worked in Piraeus with other Greek ex-servicemen unloading ship timber, until a friendship he had struck up with a French sea captain enabled him to get to Marseille. Thanks to his military uniform, he traveled by train to Paris and on to Brussels, where employees at the Greek embassy directed him to his parents' home at 70, Rue du Pont. The door was opened by his sister Hermione, who did not recognize him: she had been only six years old when he left Tire. At first his parents did not know him either, until he spoke to them, and then they wept and so did he. After a few days rest, Nicias got a job blending tobacco in Maastricht's Der Mund plant. On New Year's Eve, 1925, as he and his brothers were dining in a restaurant on the Grande Place in Brussels, they fell into conversation with the people at the next table, one of whom was the son of the Mexican consul and spoke of the wonders of his country. The next day, January 1, 1926, Nicias told his family that he was going to Mexico. Having spent seven years in the army, he had no wish to be confined from eight to ten hours a day in a factory. His parents pleaded with him, protesting that if he went away they would never see him again. They were right. On February 4 he sailed from Antwerp on the Dutch boat *Esdam* to Veracruz, where he disembarked one month later to the day. Soon after his arrival, Nicias, now in Michoacán state, met Josefina Fuentes, a native of Contepec. They married and had eight children, five boys and three girls, the latter deceased in infancy. Penelope and Theologos passed away during the 1930s, and are buried in Brussels Municipal Cemetery. When Nicias's brother Cleomenis traveled back to Tire, he found the parental home full of holes where the Turks had been digging for any valuables the Greeks might have buried before departing. Nicias never returned to Smyrna, to Greece, or to Europe.

Acknowledgments

All through my childhood in Contepec, Michoacán, my father, Nicias Aridjis Theologos, often spoke to us about the catastrophe of Asia Minor and the massacre of Greeks and Armenians in 1922. Some of the events and details included in the present work were taken from the memoirs he wrote for his children, and from his conversation.

I have also consulted the accounts of the event left to us by eye-witnesses such as George Horton, consul-general of the United States and author of *The Blight of Asia*. In 1926 he wrote that Ionia was "the land of the Seven Cities of the Revelation, of the Seven Churches and the wonderful mystical poem of St. John the Divine. Six of the candles went out in eternal darkness long ago, but that of Smyrna burned brightly until its destruction on the thirteenth of September, 1922, by the Turks of Mustapha Kemal."

Among other sources, I have drawn on information provided by Arthur Hepburn, captain of USS *Lawrence*; *La mort de Smyrne*, by René Puaux; *The Smyrna Holocaust*, by Rev. Charles Dobson; The *Martyrdom of Smyrna and Eastern Christendom*, by Dr. Lysimachos Oeconomos; and *La vérité sur un drame historique: La catastrophe de Smyrne, septembre 1922,* by Evdokimos Dourmoussis. Last but not least, I read *The Smyrna Affair*, by Marjorie Housepian; *Paradise Lost: Smyrna, 1922*, by Giles Milton; *A Blue Sea of Blood: Deciphering the Mysterious Fate of* USS *Edsall*, by Donald M. Kehn Jr.; and various translations of *The Iliad* and *The Odyssey*.

Lou Ureneck's *The Great Fire*, also known as *Smyrna September 1922*, has been especially useful in preparing the American translation of my book.

With respect to the poems of C. P. Cavafy, I have used the English translations by Edmund Keeley and Philip Sherrard. I have also consulted the dispatches filed by North American and British journalists in September 1922, and the consular documents compiled by George Horton in *Report on Turkey*, an indispensable historical text for understanding those terrible days. Sources I have treated with caution include the tendentious dispatches of Mark Bristol, the US high commissioner in Constantinople, the frivolous reportage of Ernest Hemingway, and accounts by Western vultures of history such as Pierre Loti and his followers, some of whom have dared contend that "the Greeks burned Smyrna to burn themselves."

Almost a hundred years after the atrocities committed by Kemalist forces against Christians; before the demented pyromania of those who reduced Smyrna, the City of Tolerance, to ashes, along with its inhabitants; before the delirium of destruction that possessed the Turks during those days in September 1922, I still cannot find the words to explain, to myself or to others, the Turkish genocide of Asia Minor.

About the Author

The youngest of five brothers, Homero Aridjis was born in 1940 in the village of Contepec, Michoacán, Mexico, to a Mexican mother and a Greek father. He began writing at the age of eleven, after surviving an accident that nearly cost him his life. He won a scholarship from the Mexican Writers' Center at the age of nineteen, and in 1964 was the youngest-ever recipient of the Xavier Villaurrutia Prize for best book of the year, for *Mirándola dormir* (*Watching Her Sleep*), a classic of erotic poetry. After two years in Europe on a Guggenheim fellowship, he taught at Indiana and New York Universities before entering the Mexican diplomatic service, becoming ambassador to Switzerland and then The Netherlands while still in his thirties. Before returning to Mexico, he held a second Guggenheim fellowship and was writer-in-residence at Columbia University. In 1985 Aridjis and ninety-nine other renowned artists and intellectuals founded the legendary Grupo de los Cien, an organization that addresses national and international environmental and ethical issues. In 2002 he held the Nichols Chair in Humanities and the Public Sphere at the University of Califoria, Irvine. He served two terms as president of PEN International between 1997 and 2003, during which he strove to make PEN less Eurocentric. Aridjis was Mexico's ambassador to UNESCO from 2007 until 2010, and since then has lived in Mexico City.

In addition to nineteen volumes of poetry and seventeen novels, Aridjis has written fifteen children's books, short story collections, essays, and plays, and for many years was an editorial page columnist for the Mexican newspapers *La Jornada* and *Reforma*. His work has been translated into fifteen languages and recognized with literary prizes, such as the Grinzane Cavour, for the Italian translation of *1492: The Life and Times of Juan Cabezón of Castile*. In 1997 he received the Prix Roger Caillois in France for the ensemble of his work, and in 2002 the Smederevo Golden Key poetry prize. In 2013, 2016, and 2019 translations of two recent books received international poetry awards in Italy. A wide-ranging bilingual anthology of his poetry was published in England (2001) and the United States (2002) under the title, *Eyes to See Otherwise: Ojos de otro mirar*. In 2012 *Tiempo de ángeles/A Time of Angels* was published by Fondo de Cultura Económica and City Lights. Other books in English include *Persephone*, *The Lord of the Last Day: Visions of the Year 1000*, *Solar Poems*, *The Child Poet*, *Maria the Monarch*, and *News of the Earth*, an autobiography of his relationship with the natural world through his extensive writings and thirty-three years of activism.

A champion of gray whales, monarch butterflies, sea turtles, and rain forests, Aridjis has been called the "green conscience" of his country. His passionate defense of the Earth has been acknowledged with numerous international awards, including the UNEP Global 500 Award, the Orion Society's John Hay Award, and the Millennial Award for International Environmental Leadership, given by Mikhail Gorbachev and Global Green.